The Untold Story of the Challenger Explosion:

A Journey Through Time, Conspiracy

Author: Dr. Cassandra Holt

The Untold Story of the Challenger Explosion: A Journey Through Time, Conspiracy

David Moore and Dr. Cassandra Holt

Published by Dr. Cassandra Holt, 2024.

THE UNTOLD STORY OF THE CHALLENGER EXPLOSION: A JOURNEY THROUGH TIME, CONSPIRACY

First edition. September 20, 2024.

Copyright © 2024 David Moore and Dr. Cassandra Holt.

ISBN: 979-8227472458

Written by David Moore and Dr. Cassandra Holt.

To the brave crew of the *Challenger*, whose courage and spirit will forever inspire us to reach for the stars. And to those who quietly carry the weight of sacrifice, whose stories may never be told but whose impact echoes through time.

This is for you.

Chapter 1: Shadows in the Stars

The 1980s were a decade of ambition for NASA. With the Space Shuttle program in full swing, the agency had promised the American public and the world a new era of space exploration—one that was not only exciting but routine. Space would no longer be an exclusive domain for the highly trained and elite few. Now, teachers, civilians, and ordinary people could join the ranks of those who ventured beyond Earth's atmosphere.

NASA's public vision was bold: reusable space shuttles, more frequent missions, and a future where space travel became as commonplace as air travel. The Space Shuttle was the symbol of that dream—a technological marvel that captured the hearts and imaginations of millions. However, beneath the gleaming surface of space exploration, unseen forces were at play. Hidden political pressures from government officials, corporate sponsors, and military interests placed an enormous burden on NASA.

Congressional funding for NASA was in constant jeopardy, and every mission had become a test of the agency's ability to deliver on its promises. The budget cuts of the 1970s had forced NASA to make compromises, and by the 1980s, the agency was struggling to maintain its lofty goals. Behind closed doors, top NASA officials fought to keep their program alive, knowing that failure could mean the end of America's space dominance.

But it wasn't just about funding. The Space Shuttle missions, while presented as civilian achievements, were deeply entwined with military objectives. Classified payloads and experimental military technology were frequently aboard the shuttles, and the lines between peaceful exploration and strategic advantage were becoming blurred. In the shadows, powerful figures pushed for more aggressive timelines, even as engineers warned of the risks. The Shuttle program had to succeed, no matter the cost.

As NASA prepared for the Challenger mission, these pressures were mounting. The public was excited about Christa McAuliffe, the first teacher in space, but behind the scenes, tensions were high. There were whispers of strange anomalies in the telemetry from previous missions, and concerns about the integrity of the shuttle's aging components. Yet, none of these warning signs were enough to delay what was being touted as NASA's most important mission yet.

In the quiet hallways of NASA headquarters, some began to wonder if they were pushing too far, too fast. The bold vision for space exploration had become entangled in a web of political games, financial desperation, and the unknown dangers lurking in the vastness of space.

Chapter 2: The Secret Committee

In the hidden corners of the U.S. government, far from the press releases and public excitement surrounding the Space Shuttle program, there existed a group known only to a select few as "The Oversight Committee." It was an unofficial branch, not recognized on any NASA organizational chart, yet its influence ran deep. Formed during the Cold War as a response to Soviet advancements in space and technology, the Committee's mandate was clear: protect American space superiority at all costs.

Officially, the Committee's role was to assess the risks of high-stakes space missions and ensure national security interests were safeguarded. Unofficially, they were tasked with handling the unexplainable—anomalies and data irregularities that traditional science struggled to explain. Over the years, they had quietly intervened in missions when strange signals or unexplained phenomena appeared on radar or telemetry reports, and their presence had grown as the Space Shuttle program progressed.

In the months leading up to the Challenger mission, the Committee had been on high alert. Since the early days of shuttle flights, there had been unusual data showing up in the system logs—small, seemingly inconsequential glitches at first, but they began to form a pattern. Transmissions would briefly cut out, instruments would report impossible readings, and anomalies would flash across the monitors for split seconds before vanishing.

At first, NASA dismissed these as technical bugs, the natural hiccups of new and complex technology. However, when a particularly disturbing incident occurred on the third shuttle flight, the Committee began to take a closer look. During re-entry, the shuttle's telemetry recorded an unidentifiable signal that didn't correspond with any known technology, either terrestrial or celestial. No one could explain where it came from or what it meant, but it was quickly buried within the classified files of the Committee.

The scientists within NASA were not informed. To them, everything continued as normal, their concerns focused on mechanical safety and the everyday stresses of space travel. But for the Committee, these incidents pointed to something deeper—an unknown factor influencing space missions in ways they couldn't fully understand.

As the Challenger launch date neared, the Committee held a closed-door meeting. Inside a nondescript government building, far from NASA's Houston hub, a group of high-ranking officials and analysts pored over the latest data. The unexplainable signals were growing more frequent, especially in the Challenger's launch windows. Satellite readings and ground-based sensors had started to pick up what looked like faint, erratic distortions—tiny rifts in space, mere blips, but enough to suggest something unusual was happening in Earth's upper atmosphere.

There was talk of anomalies being linked to certain orbital paths, or perhaps remnants of past missions leaving residual energy behind. Yet, more radical theories circulated among the Committee's inner circle: Was there something about Earth's space missions that was triggering a response from beyond? Some whispered that these anomalies were more than just technical glitches—they were signals, maybe even warnings.

One member of the Committee, a former aerospace engineer with ties to black projects, voiced a concern that lingered in the room: "What if we've been poking into areas we shouldn't? Space is vast, and we don't understand everything out there. What if something is watching?"

Despite their mounting unease, the decision was made not to intervene publicly. To cancel the Challenger mission would draw too much attention and raise too many questions. The media circus surrounding Christa McAuliffe's journey into space made any delay or postponement politically unfeasible. But behind the scenes, the Committee authorized enhanced surveillance, dispatching a covert team to monitor the launch from classified locations.

As the meeting adjourned, the Committee's chairperson lingered behind, staring at the most recent data anomaly on the screen. It was a brief pulse, recorded during a routine pre-flight test, lasting less than a second. But within that fraction of time, the signal had spiked to impossible levels before disappearing again.

"What are we missing?" the chairperson muttered, a chill settling over the room.

The wheels of the Challenger mission continued to turn, oblivious to the questions that lingered in the minds of those in the Committee. For them, the explosion wasn't just a risk—it was becoming a growing possibility that something far more mysterious, far more dangerous, was about to unfold.

Chapter 3: A Glitch in Time

The lead-up to the Challenger launch was supposed to be routine. Engineers and scientists at NASA had done this countless times—every bolt, every wire, every computer system was checked and double-checked. But as the Challenger mission approached, strange things began happening, anomalies that defied logical explanation.

It started small. During a routine systems test on the shuttle, a group of engineers at Kennedy Space Center noticed an irregularity in the telemetry. Data streams, which were usually precise and steady, had brief but noticeable spikes. Just milliseconds long, they appeared on the diagnostic systems as tiny blips—too fast to analyze in real-time, but just long enough to leave a record.

At first, no one thought much of it. Space shuttle systems were incredibly complex, and glitches were not unheard of in pre-launch testing. The engineers ran their checks again, dismissing the anomaly as a technical error. However, when the tests were repeated the next day, the same thing happened. Only this time, the spikes were larger.

Roger, one of the senior engineers overseeing the telemetry, took a closer look. He'd seen strange readings before, but there was something unsettling about this. The pattern didn't fit any known malfunction or typical interference. It was as if something external, something invisible, was momentarily interacting with the shuttle's systems. The data fluctuations weren't coming from within the shuttle—they were originating from outside sources, but no one could pinpoint what or where.

"Run it again," Roger ordered, his brow furrowed with growing concern.

They ran the tests for a third time. As Challenger's systems went through their diagnostic routine, Roger and his team watched the telemetry closely. This time, the blip didn't just spike. The readings flatlined for precisely 0.73 seconds—long enough for everyone in the room to notice, long enough to send shivers down their spines. And then the data snapped back, as if nothing had happened.

"What the hell was that?" someone muttered from the back of the room.

Roger couldn't answer. They ran the tests again, but the glitch didn't reappear. It was as if that moment, those 0.73 seconds, had simply been erased from time. No explanation was given, and no system on the shuttle showed signs of failure.

It wasn't just telemetry either. Other systems were acting oddly. A minor malfunction in the shuttle's flight control system required a reset. The shuttle's internal clocks showed brief desynchronizations during tests—fractions of a second, but noticeable. It was as though time itself had hiccuped.

Roger knew something wasn't right, and he wasn't the only one. He exchanged quiet words with other engineers, some of whom had seen similar anomalies in previous shuttle missions. These weren't normal glitches. Something was interfering with the shuttle's systems, and it wasn't coming from the shuttle itself.

Later that day, Roger sat down with a colleague, Sarah, who had been working on monitoring the external communication systems. She had a theory—one she hesitated to share.

"You ever hear of temporal distortion?" she asked, her voice low.

Roger blinked. "Like time travel? Come on, Sarah, we're engineers, not sci-fi writers."

"I know, I know," she said, leaning in. "But what if these glitches aren't mechanical? What if they're... something else? Something outside our normal understanding of physics?"

Roger scoffed at first but couldn't shake the nagging feeling that Sarah might be onto something. The telemetry anomalies weren't behaving like any electrical interference or software bug. And the precise, recurring 0.73-second gap couldn't be a coincidence.

That evening, Roger returned to his desk and reviewed telemetry logs from previous shuttle missions. His stomach tightened as he noticed a disturbing trend. In every mission he examined, there were similar glitches. Each one brief, seemingly harmless, and easily overlooked. But now, in the light of Challenger's upcoming mission, they appeared connected—like pieces of a puzzle no one had realized they were assembling.

Worse still, as he dug deeper, Roger found references to an older, classified report—one that dated back to the Apollo program. There had been similar glitches back then too, dismissed as random noise in the data. But now, it seemed there was more to the story.

Roger's heart raced as he came to a troubling conclusion: these glitches weren't isolated. They had been happening for years, hidden in the data of America's space program. And with the Challenger mission, they were becoming more frequent, more pronounced.

What if the Challenger wasn't just a victim of technical failure waiting to happen? What if something—something they didn't fully understand—was affecting the shuttle? Something outside the realm of conventional science.

Roger decided to quietly compile all his findings and report them to his superiors, but in the back of his mind, he knew this would be met with skepticism. NASA couldn't afford to delay the Challenger mission over vague telemetry glitches. The political pressure was immense, and the launch date was locked in.

But as he stared at the blip in the data—those 0.73 seconds that seemed to vanish into nothing—Roger couldn't shake the feeling that time itself was being bent, manipulated by forces far beyond their control. Forces that no one, not even the best engineers in the world, were prepared to confront.

As the Challenger crew prepared for their historic flight, an invisible danger loomed. One that no one could explain, but that everyone would soon feel.

Chapter 4: The Chosen Crew

The Challenger crew had been chosen not only for their skills and expertise but for the hope they represented. They were the embodiment of NASA's bold vision for space exploration and the spirit of innovation that the shuttle program promised. While each astronaut had their own story, it was Christa McAuliffe—the teacher from Concord, New Hampshire—who captured the hearts of the American people.

NASA's decision to include a civilian, and specifically a schoolteacher, on this mission wasn't just about breaking new ground; it was about reigniting public interest in space exploration. The space program, once the pinnacle of national pride, had begun to lose its luster in the eyes of the public. The allure of space travel had dimmed, and NASA needed something—someone—to bring the excitement back.

Christa McAuliffe was that someone. As the first civilian chosen to go to space, she represented every teacher, every student, and every dreamer who looked to the stars and imagined the impossible. Her mission, "Teacher in Space," was designed to engage millions of schoolchildren, and her lessons from space were to be broadcast live to classrooms across the country. It was an unprecedented moment in NASA's history, and McAuliffe was the face of it.

But behind the media frenzy and public spotlight, each of the Challenger crew members carried their own stories, their own hopes, and their own sacrifices.

Commander Francis R. Scobee was a decorated Air Force veteran and seasoned pilot. He had flown helicopters in Vietnam and logged thousands of hours in various aircraft before joining NASA. To him, the Challenger mission wasn't just another flight; it was the culmination of a lifetime's work. Scobee had always believed in pushing boundaries, and his calm demeanor and leadership made him a natural choice to command this crucial mission.

Pilot Michael J. Smith, a Naval aviator with a strong technical background, was Scobee's right-hand man. Smith was known for his sharp mind and steady hand in high-pressure situations. He had flown over 4,000 hours in various aircraft and had served as a test pilot, making him a perfect fit for the Challenger's high-profile mission. Though new to space, Smith had always dreamed of the stars and saw this mission as his chance to leave a mark on history.

Mission Specialist Judith A. Resnik, an accomplished engineer and one of the few female astronauts in NASA's ranks, brought a unique blend of intellect and determination to the crew. Resnik had flown before on the Discovery mission and was no stranger to the challenges of spaceflight. As one of the first women in space, she was a trailblazer, admired for her tenacity and brilliance. Her role on Challenger was critical, overseeing the shuttle's scientific experiments and ensuring that everything ran smoothly in orbit.

Ellison S. Onizuka, another mission specialist, was a proud son of Hawaii and the first Asian-American astronaut. Onizuka had a fierce pride in his heritage and had worked tirelessly to overcome the barriers that had once seemed insurmountable. He had flown on the Discovery mission alongside Resnik and was excited to continue his journey with NASA. Onizuka was set to oversee satellite deployment on the Challenger mission, a task that would bring him one step closer to his lifelong dream of space exploration.

Ronald McNair, physicist, engineer, and mission specialist, was another groundbreaking figure on the crew. Growing up in the segregated South, McNair had faced enormous odds in his journey to NASA. His fierce determination and intellect led him to MIT, where he earned his Ph.D. in physics. He was deeply committed to using his platform to inspire young African Americans to pursue careers in science and technology. On Challenger, McNair was tasked with operating scientific equipment and conducting experiments in space.

And then there was **Gregory Jarvis**, payload specialist, whose job was to oversee the satellite deployment and other payload operations. Jarvis had trained diligently for this mission, understanding the critical role the satellite would play in future telecommunications. Like the others, he had spent years preparing for this moment, dreaming of the stars and the weightlessness of space.

Finally, there was Christa McAuliffe. Though she had no military or aerospace background like her fellow crew members, her place on the Challenger was just as important. She was selected from over 11,000 applicants for the Teacher in Space Program, a nationwide search that had captured the imagination of millions. McAuliffe was an ordinary person about to embark on an extraordinary journey, and that's what made her special.

To her students, Christa McAuliffe was a dedicated teacher who believed in the power of education to change the world. She had spent her career inspiring young minds, and now she would be doing it on a global scale. Her lesson plans were ready, her enthusiasm infectious. She knew she was a symbol—a representative of educators everywhere—and she embraced that responsibility with grace and humility.

Despite the excitement surrounding her mission, McAuliffe couldn't ignore the slight sense of unease that lingered in the background. As she completed her rigorous training, she learned more about the challenges and dangers of spaceflight than she had ever anticipated. Still, her optimism never wavered. She believed deeply in the mission, in NASA, and in the promise of space exploration.

As launch day approached, the Challenger crew bonded in ways only astronauts could understand. They had trained together for months, supported each other through the highs and lows, and shared the weight of the mission's success on their shoulders. Each member carried their own dreams, and together they represented the best of what humanity could achieve.

However, even as they made final preparations for launch, none of them could have anticipated the invisible forces at play behind the scenes—forces that would forever change the course of their mission and their lives.

The Challenger crew was ready for their journey into the stars, unaware that this voyage would take them into the annals of history, not for the reasons they hoped, but for reasons they could never imagine.

Chapter 5: The Classified Briefing

The meeting took place in a small, nondescript room deep within NASA's Johnson Space Center, far from the bustling activity of mission control. The atmosphere was thick with tension, and as the top engineers filed in, they exchanged uneasy glances. This was no ordinary briefing. They had all received the summons earlier that morning, instructing them to attend a classified meeting under strict non-disclosure agreements. The content was described only as "critical to national security and future missions."

Once everyone had taken their seats, the room fell into a tense silence. At the front of the room stood a man none of them had seen before—sharp, stern, with an air of authority that suggested he wasn't from NASA. His dark suit and government-issued ID badge were enough to tell them he was part of an outside agency, but which one remained a mystery.

"Good afternoon," he began, his voice steady but grave. "What you're about to hear is classified at the highest level. This information has been tightly controlled for the past several years, but due to recent developments, we believe it is necessary to bring a select group of NASA personnel into the fold. You have been chosen because of your expertise and your roles in the upcoming Challenger mission."

The engineers shifted in their seats, exchanging worried looks. What could possibly be so urgent? They had all been neck-deep in preparing for Challenger's launch, and this briefing, so close to launch day, felt like a disruption they didn't need.

The man gestured to a projector screen behind him, which flickered to life with grainy footage from a previous shuttle mission. The timestamp in the corner indicated it was from 1984, the *Discovery* mission. The engineers recognized the footage immediately—it was from the shuttle's ascent into orbit.

"We've been monitoring a series of anomalies over the last several shuttle flights," the man explained, his eyes scanning the room as if gauging their reactions. "What you're about to see was picked up during *Discovery's* mission two years ago. This has never been released to the public."

The video showed the shuttle gliding smoothly through space. For a few moments, it appeared to be standard footage, with nothing out of the ordinary. Then, suddenly, a sharp blip appeared on the screen—a bright, pulsing signal that seemed to come from nowhere, just outside the shuttle's field of view. It lasted for less than a second, but in that brief flash, the instruments aboard *Discovery* had recorded something they couldn't explain.

"This is the signal," the man continued, his tone cold and measured. "It doesn't match any known frequency used by terrestrial or satellite technology. What's more concerning is that it was picked up by multiple sensors on the shuttle's exterior. We've since reviewed data from previous missions and found similar anomalies dating back to the early shuttle flights, though none as strong as this."

One of the engineers, a systems specialist named Tom, leaned forward, his brows knit with concern. "So... what exactly are we looking at here? An interference from another satellite? Cosmic radiation?"

The man shook his head. "No. This isn't natural interference, and it's not from any man-made source. In fact, we've run it through every known classification system, and it doesn't match anything. We believe this is an extraterrestrial signal."

A heavy silence fell over the room as the word "extraterrestrial" hung in the air like a cold weight. Several of the engineers exchanged skeptical looks, their rational minds struggling to process what they were hearing.

Another engineer, Sarah—who had been on edge ever since noticing the strange telemetry glitches during Challenger's tests—spoke up. "You're telling us that this signal, whatever it is, has been out there for years, and we're only learning about it now?"

The man's expression didn't change. "We had reasons to keep this information compartmentalized. The signal is erratic, difficult to track, and up until recently, we didn't consider it an immediate threat. But over the past few months, we've noticed something alarming. The anomalies are becoming more frequent, and they're centered around the Challenger launch window."

A ripple of shock passed through the room. Tom shook his head in disbelief. "Are you saying the Challenger mission is being... targeted? By whatever this signal is?"

"We don't know," the man admitted. "What we do know is that the signal seems to be increasing in strength, and it's more concentrated around certain shuttle launch windows. We believe it may have something to do with the trajectory Challenger will be following."

Another voice, this time from Roger, one of the lead engineers on the Challenger project, cut through the tension. "So what are we supposed to do about this? Delay the launch? Investigate further? I don't think we can just ignore something like this."

The man's face remained impassive. "Unfortunately, delaying the launch is not an option. The political and public pressures surrounding the Challenger mission make it too high-profile to halt at this stage. However, we are enhancing surveillance measures, and we'll be monitoring for any signs of interference once the shuttle is in orbit. We're asking you to continue your work as planned but remain vigilant. If any more anomalies appear in the data, report them immediately to this committee—no one else."

The weight of the situation began to settle in, and the engineers could feel the gravity of what they were being asked. They had spent their entire careers believing in the reliability of their calculations, their systems, and their understanding of the universe. But this—this was something beyond all of that.

As the briefing concluded and the engineers filed out of the room, the man stayed behind, watching them leave with a guarded expression. For NASA, the Challenger mission had become a symbol of inspiration and progress. For the government operatives behind the classified briefing, it was a potential flashpoint—one that could reveal forces far beyond their control.

Sarah walked alongside Roger as they left, her mind racing. "Do you believe any of this?" she asked in a hushed voice.

Roger shook his head slowly. "I don't know what to believe anymore. But if there's something out there, watching us... and if it's been affecting our missions for years... then we're in way over our heads."

As the engineers returned to their workstations, the knowledge of the classified briefing weighed heavily on their minds. The upcoming Challenger mission was no longer just a technological or scientific achievement. It was now tangled in a web of mystery, uncertainty, and a threat they barely understood.

And as launch day loomed closer, one question lingered in everyone's mind: What was waiting for them beyond the atmosphere?

Chapter 6: O-Rings and Warnings

As the countdown to the Challenger launch continued, NASA's engineers worked tirelessly to ensure every detail of the shuttle was ready. However, amidst the growing excitement, one voice stood out—Roger Boisjoly, a senior engineer at Morton Thiokol, the contractor responsible for the shuttle's solid rocket boosters. For months, Roger had been raising alarms about a critical component of the shuttle: the O-rings. These small rubber seals, located between sections of the solid rocket boosters, were designed to prevent hot gases from escaping during launch. But under certain conditions—particularly cold temperatures—Roger feared they might fail.

The warnings came after several internal tests revealed concerning data. During cold weather simulations, the O-rings displayed reduced elasticity, causing them to harden and fail to form a proper seal. If they failed during launch, there was a high risk of a catastrophic event. Roger had seen the results firsthand, and the prospect of such a failure weighed heavily on his conscience.

Despite his repeated concerns, the urgency of the situation wasn't fully acknowledged. NASA's schedule was tight, and pressure from both the government and the public made delays unthinkable. The Challenger mission was more than just another flight—it was a symbol of the future, a beacon of hope that had captured the nation's imagination. Christa McAuliffe's participation as the first civilian, a teacher, was central to NASA's narrative. The mission had to succeed.

In the days leading up to the launch, Roger and his team continued to push for a delay. The weather forecast predicted unusually cold temperatures on the morning of January 28, 1986—far colder than any previous shuttle launch. Boisjoly was adamant: the O-rings were not designed to function properly in such conditions. He knew that if they didn't seal correctly, the high-pressure gas from the solid rocket boosters could leak, ignite, and lead to disaster.

However, behind the scenes, NASA faced even more troubling uncertainties than the O-rings. Roger's warnings, though grounded in engineering logic, were overshadowed by the lingering fears of something far more dangerous—something unknown. Since the classified briefing, whispers had circulated among NASA's upper echelons about the unexplained signals and anomalies detected during shuttle flights. The extraterrestrial signal from the *Discovery* mission two years earlier remained an enigma, and now, in the days leading up to Challenger's launch, similar anomalies were reappearing in telemetry data.

Among those who knew of the classified information, there was an unspoken dread that something was watching. The strange signals, erratic telemetry, and classified warnings were beginning to coalesce into a larger picture. Some believed the O-ring issue was only part of the problem—something they could fix with engineering solutions. But what about the unexplained forces lurking just beyond Earth's atmosphere?

At a crucial meeting on the evening of January 27, Roger Boisjoly once again presented his data to NASA and Morton Thiokol executives. He was joined by fellow engineers, all of whom shared his concerns about the O-rings. "We are risking lives if we go forward with this launch under these conditions," Roger said, his voice firm yet exhausted from the constant battle. He laid out his evidence: test results, simulations, and worst-case scenarios. The data was clear—the O-rings were likely to fail in the cold weather.

For a moment, there was a heavy silence in the room. The engineers had made their case. But then came the response. NASA managers, under pressure to keep the schedule on track, pushed back. The launch had already been delayed several times due to technical issues and weather concerns. The political ramifications of another delay, especially with Christa McAuliffe and the media frenzy surrounding her flight, were enormous.

The decision was made to proceed.

Roger left the meeting with a sinking feeling in his chest. His warnings had been overruled, his data dismissed. He knew that the temperature on launch day would be dangerously low, and there was nothing more he could do. He feared for the worst, but in the face of bureaucratic and public pressure, his voice had been lost.

While the engineers prepared for launch, the deeper fear—the one hidden behind classified doors—loomed. Inside NASA, a small group of officials continued to monitor the strange signals they had been tracking. In the days leading up to the launch, the erratic telemetry spikes had appeared again, following a pattern that no one could fully explain. Even stranger, these anomalies seemed to intensify as the shuttle's launch window approached.

There was no concrete proof that these signals had any direct connection to the Challenger, but for those few who knew the truth, there was a creeping dread that something more than just mechanical failure might be at play.

As the morning of January 28th dawned, the cold air gripped Cape Canaveral. Frost covered the shuttle's exterior, and the temperature was far below anything NASA had ever launched in before. Roger watched from a distance, his heart heavy with the knowledge of the risks. The engineers at Morton Thiokol were silent, knowing they had done all they could to warn NASA about the O-rings.

Yet, for all the concern about the mechanical integrity of the shuttle, the engineers had no knowledge of the far greater mystery—one hidden in classified briefings and unsolved anomalies. For some at NASA, there was an uneasy feeling that something beyond human understanding was at work, something beyond the physical limitations of rubber seals and mechanical failures.

As the countdown clock ticked toward zero, the world watched with eager anticipation. For most, it was the start of another great chapter in space exploration. For a few, it was the culmination of fears that had been growing ever since the first signal was detected.

But as Roger Boisjoly stood silently, bracing for what he feared might happen, he couldn't have known that his concerns about the O-rings were only part of the larger equation—an equation that included not only mechanical failure but forces far beyond anything NASA had ever prepared for.

Chapter 7: Anomalous Readings

The pre-launch buzz at Kennedy Space Center was electric on the morning of January 28, 1986. Engineers, technicians, and NASA officials hustled to complete the final checks on the Challenger space shuttle as the crew prepared for their historic mission. The crisp Florida air, unusually cold for this time of year, brought an unsettling chill over the launch site, but for most, the excitement of the mission far outweighed the unease.

However, deep within NASA's network of satellite monitoring stations and ground-based radar facilities, a small team of specialists was growing increasingly concerned. In the days leading up to the launch, they had been tracking something unusual—anomalies that didn't fit with any known weather patterns or satellite interference. At first, the readings had been intermittent, small distortions that appeared and disappeared too quickly to draw definitive conclusions. But as the launch day approached, the anomalies became more frequent and more pronounced.

It began with a signal from a weather satellite orbiting over the Atlantic Ocean. The satellite, tasked with providing atmospheric data to assist with launch preparations, recorded a brief spike in radiation levels near the Challenger launch site—just off the Florida coast. The spike lasted only a second, but it was far higher than anything the satellite had ever recorded. The readings indicated a concentrated burst of energy that couldn't be attributed to natural causes, such as solar flares or geomagnetic storms.

At first, the technicians overseeing the satellite data assumed it was a technical glitch, similar to those seen in earlier missions. But when the anomaly repeated itself a few hours later, they grew suspicious. The energy spike had moved, now hovering closer to the launch site and lingering longer than before. It was as if something was approaching, slowly but steadily.

Simultaneously, ground-based radar stations picked up faint but unmistakable interference in the atmosphere above the Cape Canaveral area. The radar operators, used to monitoring for aircraft and weather systems, were perplexed. The interference appeared as a distortion, almost like a tear in the atmosphere—something they had never seen before. It didn't correspond with any aircraft, nor was it related to the cold front that had brought freezing temperatures to the area.

The radar operators flagged the anomaly and escalated it to higher-ups within NASA's launch operations division. The response was swift, but not what they expected. A senior official quickly shut down any discussion of the anomaly, instructing the radar team to continue monitoring but not to raise any further alarms. It was an order that left the radar technicians uneasy, as they were certain something unusual was happening in the skies over Challenger's launch site.

Elsewhere, inside a secure control room at Vandenberg Air Force Base in California, classified surveillance satellites—part of a joint military-NASA program—picked up something even more disturbing. One of the satellites, designed to detect foreign spacecraft and missile launches, recorded an unexplained object in low Earth orbit. The object wasn't part of any known satellite constellation, and it moved in a way that defied the typical orbital patterns of man-made spacecraft. Even stranger, its trajectory appeared to intersect with the Challenger's planned flight path.

The operators at Vandenberg quickly relayed the information to a secretive NASA committee responsible for monitoring anomalies during space missions—the same committee that had been briefed on the extraterrestrial signals detected during earlier shuttle flights. For the committee, this new data added a troubling layer to an already precarious situation. There were too many coincidences: the unexplained energy bursts, the radar distortions, and now an unidentified object in orbit.

As the data poured in, the atmosphere within the committee grew tense. They knew that delaying the Challenger launch to investigate further would raise too many questions. The political stakes were too high, and the public excitement around the mission, with Christa McAuliffe set to become the first teacher in space, made any delay unthinkable.

One member of the committee, a senior physicist named Dr. Allan Hayes, reviewed the satellite data in silence. He had been involved in analyzing the mysterious signals detected during previous shuttle missions and was all too familiar with the strange readings that had plagued NASA's spaceflights. For years, he had pushed for a deeper investigation into the anomalies, but his concerns were always brushed aside as too speculative, too abstract.

Now, as he stared at the radar distortion over the Challenger's launch site and the unidentified object moving closer in orbit, he felt a sinking realization. These anomalies weren't isolated incidents—they were connected, part of a larger phenomenon that no one could explain. And they were happening with greater frequency.

Dr. Hayes called an emergency meeting of the committee, briefing them on the latest findings. The room was filled with grim faces as he laid out the evidence. "We can't ignore this," he said, his voice steady but urgent. "There's something out there. It's been watching us for years, and now it's getting closer. Whatever it is, it's affecting our missions. We need to take this seriously before it's too late."

The committee members exchanged nervous glances. They were scientists and engineers, trained to deal with the tangible and the measurable, but this—this was different. There was no concrete proof that the anomalies posed an immediate threat to the Challenger mission, but the sheer volume of unexplained data was hard to ignore.

Yet, as the launch time approached, the decision was made to proceed. The anomalies were quietly documented and filed away in classified reports. Officially, the Challenger mission was going forward without any known issues.

On the morning of the launch, as the countdown ticked down, the anomalies continued. Ground stations reported increased interference, and the unidentified object in orbit remained in its strange, unpredictable trajectory. No one dared raise the alarm. The Challenger launch was too important, too public, and the risks, while alarming to some, were not considered imminent.

But as the shuttle stood on the launch pad, with the crew ready for liftoff, those who knew the truth could feel the weight of something unseen pressing down on them. Roger Boisjoly's concerns about the O-rings were valid, but to those aware of the anomalous readings, the danger went far beyond mechanical failure.

In those final moments, when the world's attention was fixed on the launch, the atmosphere around Challenger seemed charged with something otherworldly—an energy that couldn't be measured by conventional means.

And as the engines ignited and the shuttle roared to life, the anomalies continued to hum, silently watching, as if waiting for the moment when everything would change.

Chapter 8: The Specter of Apollo

The tension surrounding the Challenger launch brought back memories of the Apollo missions for a select few within NASA—memories they had hoped would remain buried. For years, the agency had carefully curated the narrative of the Apollo program, presenting it as one of humankind's greatest achievements: landing men on the moon, fulfilling President Kennedy's bold vision, and returning safely to Earth. But beneath the public triumphs lay a series of strange, unexplained incidents that never saw the light of day.

In the days leading up to the Challenger disaster, whispers of those incidents began to circulate once more among the inner circle at NASA. For the engineers and scientists working on the shuttle program, the Apollo era was seen as the golden age of space exploration. However, for those who had been involved in the darkest secrets of Apollo, the past was anything but golden—it was haunted.

In a small, dimly lit office at NASA's headquarters, a closed-door meeting was held with key officials, some of whom had been with the agency since the early Apollo days. The topic was simple yet terrifying: the strange anomalies being detected around the Challenger mission. A few senior members believed these incidents were connected to something that had first been encountered during the Apollo missions.

Dr. Arthur Connelly, one of NASA's senior mission planners during Apollo, had kept quiet for years about the odd events that had transpired in the 1960s and early 1970s. But now, as the Challenger anomalies grew more frequent, Connelly felt the past rising from the shadows. He had seen it before—the unexplained telemetry glitches, the strange signals that NASA had quietly filed away. Back then, NASA's official stance had been clear: keep it quiet. The Apollo program could not afford any distractions, especially not ones that bordered on the supernatural.

In this meeting, Connelly finally spoke of what had been hushed up decades earlier. He began by recounting one of the more infamous incidents: the unreported disturbances during Apollo 12, the second manned mission to the moon. While the mission was a success on the surface, the crew had experienced something odd during their voyage.

Midway through the journey, telemetry data recorded an unusual burst of static—a signal of unknown origin that temporarily disrupted communications between Apollo 12 and mission control. At first, it was dismissed as a solar flare or a random cosmic anomaly. But then the signal repeated itself, much stronger and far more localized. It was as though something was broadcasting directly at the Apollo spacecraft, targeting it specifically. The event was never publicly disclosed, and after much internal discussion, NASA buried the data to avoid alarming the public or fueling conspiracy theories.

The Apollo 12 crew had their own unsettling experiences. Although they stuck to the script in public, some astronauts privately shared stories of strange occurrences on the moon—flashes of light they couldn't explain, shadowy figures in their peripheral vision, and odd mechanical glitches during their moonwalks. It was enough to spook the crew, though they knew better than to raise alarm with mission control. NASA had no appetite for rumors that might derail future missions.

But Apollo 12 wasn't the only mission plagued by the unexplained.

Dr. Connelly's voice lowered as he described the most chilling case: Apollo 17, the final manned moon landing. Unlike earlier missions, Apollo 17 had encountered what the astronauts described as an "echo" in space—a persistent, rhythmic signal that seemed to mirror the shuttle's own transmissions back at them. At first, the crew assumed it was a malfunction or interference from Earth, but mission control confirmed that no such transmissions were being sent. The echo seemed to come from the void of space itself. Once again, NASA quietly dismissed the phenomenon, noting it as a benign yet unexplainable anomaly in the mission logs.

As Dr. Connelly finished recounting these incidents, the room remained silent, save for the quiet hum of the projector still displaying old Apollo data on the wall. The officials in the room knew the gravity of what was being discussed. What Connelly had revealed wasn't just old history—it was becoming relevant again.

One of the officials, Director Harold Duncan, who had risen through the ranks during the Apollo era, spoke up. "We chalked these things up to random cosmic events, unexplainable but harmless. But the truth is, we never really understood what they were. Now, with these Challenger readings... it's starting to feel like something is repeating itself."

The others nodded gravely. There was a growing suspicion that whatever had haunted the Apollo missions was now emerging once again. Only this time, it seemed to be more active, more focused.

Dr. Connelly continued, "The telemetry spikes we're seeing with Challenger, they match the patterns from Apollo 17. The same burst of static, the same energy readings—only now, the anomalies are happening more frequently, and they're stronger. Back then, we didn't have the technology to track it the way we do now, but I'm telling you, this isn't random. Something out there knows we're watching."

The room grew cold. The implications were disturbing. Were they being watched by some unknown entity? Was the very act of space exploration attracting attention from forces beyond their understanding?

NASA had always prided itself on science, logic, and reason. But now, as the anomalies mounted, some began to wonder if the very science they relied on could explain what was happening. The strange signals, the telemetry distortions, the unidentified object hovering near Challenger's flight path—none of it fit into the neat, logical boxes that NASA had built its reputation upon.

"We need to be prepared for the possibility that these anomalies aren't just random," Duncan said firmly. "If this is the same phenomenon that affected Apollo, it's possible we're dealing with something beyond our control."

There was no consensus in the room on what to do next. Officially, NASA could not delay the Challenger launch based on mysterious, unexplained readings. The public, the media, and the government were all watching, and any delay would have far-reaching consequences. But unofficially, those who knew the truth—the truth that had been buried since the Apollo days—felt an ominous presence hovering over the mission.

As the meeting ended and the officials dispersed, Dr. Connelly lingered, staring at the Apollo data one last time. He had never spoken about these incidents before, not in such detail, and now that they were resurfacing with Challenger, the dread he had long buried returned in full force.

NASA's grand missions had always been about exploration, about stepping into the unknown with courage and conviction. But what if something in that unknown had been waiting for them? What if, all these years, it had been watching, waiting for the right moment to make itself known?

And now, with Challenger, it seemed that moment was near.

Chapter 9: A World Watching

January 28, 1986. The day had finally arrived, and all eyes around the globe were fixed on Cape Canaveral, where the Challenger space shuttle stood tall on the launch pad, ready to take flight. It wasn't just another NASA mission—this one had captured the imagination of the entire world. Christa McAuliffe, a schoolteacher from New Hampshire, was about to become the first civilian to fly into space, inspiring millions of students and educators with the promise of what could be. Her participation had turned a routine shuttle launch into a global event.

News anchors in every corner of the world spoke excitedly about the historic moment. Classrooms in America had televisions wheeled in, eager children and teachers watching with anticipation. Families across Europe, Asia, and beyond gathered around their TVs, joining in the collective excitement. For many, this was a symbol of hope, progress, and humanity's boundless curiosity.

But as the countdown ticked down and the world watched with eager anticipation, hidden beneath the polished surface of NASA's public relations machine was a growing undercurrent of anxiety. Among the top brass and mission controllers, there was a palpable tension that belied the smiles and confidence projected to the outside world. Unexplained events had been unfolding in the days and hours leading up to the launch, anomalies that couldn't be ignored—yet were being kept tightly under wraps.

Inside NASA's mission control, the atmosphere was charged but nervous. The previous night had been filled with last-minute discussions, secret briefings, and quiet warnings from those in the know. Engineers like Roger Boisjoly had voiced their concerns about the O-rings, their warnings about the extreme cold conditions falling on deaf ears. Meanwhile, those who had been following the strange telemetry anomalies and radar distortions were also on edge. The unexplained readings had intensified in the hours before launch, but no one could offer a definitive explanation. For many, it felt like they were standing on the precipice of something they couldn't quite grasp.

In one of the many briefing rooms hidden away from public view, a small group of NASA officials huddled together in tense discussion. Dr. Allan Hayes, one of the key figures involved in monitoring the strange signals, stood over a series of telemetry printouts, his face etched with worry.

"The readings are getting stronger," he said in a low voice, pointing to a graph that showed a steady increase in signal strength from an unidentified source. "We've never seen it spike like this before. I don't know what it is, but it's something... something significant."

Across the table, Director Harold Duncan looked grim. "Can we delay the launch?"

Dr. Hayes shook his head. "Not without raising suspicion. We're too far in now. Any delay would create a media firestorm, and you know how the White House feels about this mission."

Duncan clenched his fists, knowing Hayes was right. The Challenger mission wasn't just a scientific endeavor—it was a political statement, a moment to reinvigorate national pride in the space program. The presence of Christa McAuliffe, the teacher-turned-astronaut, made the mission too important to cancel or delay without severe repercussions.

Outside, the media buzzed with excitement. Reporters conducted interviews with astronauts and space enthusiasts, talking up the grandeur of space exploration and the significance of this particular mission. Yet, even as they spoke of hope and progress, there were whispers of doubt from some who had caught wind of the technical issues that had plagued the shuttle.

Still, the broader public knew nothing of the anomalies, the signals, or the whispered warnings from engineers like Roger Boisjoly. They were blissfully unaware of the tensions bubbling beneath the surface.

As the minutes ticked away, families across the world tuned in for the live broadcast. In the United States, classrooms were abuzz with energy, as teachers explained the significance of Christa McAuliffe's journey. Her mission wasn't just about space exploration; it was about education, about making the stars accessible to everyone. McAuliffe had become a beacon of inspiration, embodying the belief that anyone could reach for the stars.

NASA had embraced this narrative wholeheartedly, using McAuliffe's involvement to reinvigorate interest in the space program. But behind the scenes, some of the agency's most seasoned officials couldn't shake the feeling that something was wrong.

In the control room, the countdown clock was ticking, and tension ran high. Flight Director Jay Greene kept his eyes on the monitors, his mind running through every scenario. He had heard the concerns about the O-rings, he knew about the telemetry anomalies, and he was aware of the unexplained radar disturbances. But the launch was going ahead—there was no turning back now.

As the final checks were completed, NASA's public affairs officers provided upbeat commentary for the live broadcast, their voices steady and confident. "Today, we are making history once again," one of them announced. "With Christa McAuliffe aboard, the Challenger shuttle will bring space exploration into the classroom, sparking the imaginations of millions of young minds across the globe."

But in the small classified control room where Dr. Hayes and his team monitored the strange signals, the atmosphere was anything but celebratory. A new spike had just appeared on their instruments, far stronger than before. The radar feed showed an object—unidentified, but definitely there—hovering in low Earth orbit, dangerously close to the shuttle's intended path.

"Is it debris?" someone asked.

"No," Hayes replied, his voice tight. "This is something else. Something we can't explain."

Yet, there was no time to investigate further. The countdown reached the final minutes, and the world was watching. Mission control was locked in, committed to launching the shuttle. Any delay now would be catastrophic for NASA's reputation.

The tension inside NASA was palpable, but the public would never know. The smiles, the speeches, the hopeful enthusiasm—all of it masked the anxiety brewing behind the scenes. For the engineers who had worked on the shuttle, like Roger Boisjoly, the concern was immediate and practical: the O-rings could fail. For those like Dr. Hayes and his secret team, the danger was more elusive, tied to forces they couldn't fully understand.

As the final seconds of the countdown began, the entire world held its breath. No one watching could have imagined the hidden fears, the unexplained signals, or the quiet warnings that had been whispered in the halls of NASA.

And then, with a deafening roar, the Challenger shuttle lifted off, climbing steadily into the sky. Cameras from around the world tracked its ascent, the voices of the commentators filled with excitement and pride.

But in the moments that followed, the world would be confronted with a tragedy no one could have anticipated—except for those who had been watching the signs, hidden in the shadows.

Chapter 10: The Final Countdown

January 28, 1986. The day had arrived. The countdown to the Challenger launch was nearly complete, and the excitement was palpable. From the frigid grounds of Cape Canaveral to classrooms across America and homes around the world, millions watched with bated breath as the final minutes ticked away. Christa McAuliffe, the schoolteacher set to make history, sat with her fellow astronauts, their faces hidden behind their helmets but their determination clear.

In the public eye, everything appeared flawless. NASA's iconic professionalism was on full display, and the space agency had worked tirelessly to ensure this mission would be remembered as a triumph of human ingenuity and progress. But beneath the surface, there was a tension that few could see—an unease that grew with every passing second. To those aware of the deeper complexities, this wasn't just another shuttle launch. It was a mission entangled in unexplained anomalies, technical concerns, and political pressure.

The cold morning air hung heavy over Cape Canaveral, colder than expected, colder than anything NASA had ever dealt with during a launch. Icicles clung to the launch platform, a silent testament to the temperature drop. Despite the unusual weather, the countdown continued. There was no turning back now.

In the last few hours before liftoff, the engineers at Kennedy Space Center had conducted their final checks, going over every detail one last time. Roger Boisjoly, along with his colleagues at Morton Thiokol, had tried once more to raise concerns about the O-rings. The freezing temperatures, he knew, could cause the seals to fail. But their warnings had already been dismissed by NASA management the night before. The stakes were too high to delay the mission now, and the launch schedule was already tight. Any postponement would mean an enormous financial and reputational cost.

Roger sat at his desk, watching the live feed of the shuttle on a small monitor, feeling a growing sense of dread. He had spent months fighting to address the issue, but now, with the shuttle on the launchpad, there was nothing more he could do. His gut told him that disaster was imminent, yet no one in charge had listened.

But Roger wasn't the only one troubled by what was about to happen.

In the classified control room several floors below, Dr. Allan Hayes and his team of specialists were monitoring their own set of data. The unexplained signals that had been quietly plaguing the Challenger mission for weeks were now becoming more pronounced. The energy spikes they had tracked were stronger than ever, almost as if something was building. The strange object detected in low Earth orbit remained on a collision course with the shuttle's planned flight path, though its origin and nature were still unknown.

Dr. Hayes stared at the telemetry, his mind racing. He couldn't shake the feeling that they were missing something crucial, something that couldn't be explained by the technology or science they had at their disposal. The signals, the radar anomalies, the unexplained energy readings—it all pointed to a larger, more ominous force at play, something beyond their control.

"Another spike," one of his technicians muttered, pointing at the screen. The reading showed a brief, intense burst of energy from an unknown source, concentrated in the atmosphere directly above the launch site. It was unlike anything they had seen before.

"This can't be a coincidence," Dr. Hayes said quietly, his voice tight with concern.

"What do we do?" the technician asked.

Dr. Hayes hesitated. He knew that, officially, they were not authorized to interfere. The anomalies, while concerning, had no clear explanation, and there was no concrete evidence to suggest they posed an immediate danger. But the patterns were undeniable. The signals had been growing in strength, and now they were concentrated right above the Challenger. The proximity was too close to ignore.

"We're running out of time," another team member whispered, glancing at the countdown clock.

Dr. Hayes knew they were beyond the point of stopping the launch. Even if they alerted mission control now, it would take too long to explain the anomalies, let alone justify halting a launch with such high visibility. The world was watching. Delaying the mission at this late stage would cause a media frenzy, and NASA had staked its reputation on this moment. The Challenger mission was meant to reinvigorate the space program, not stall it.

"Continue monitoring," Hayes finally ordered. "Log everything, no matter how small."

As the final seconds of the countdown began, inside the shuttle, the crew members made their last-minute adjustments, reviewing their checklists and mentally preparing for liftoff. They had trained for this moment for months, but now, with the weight of their suits pressing against them and the hum of the shuttle's systems filling their ears, the reality of what was about to happen set in.

For Christa McAuliffe, the excitement was tempered with a sense of wonder. As the first civilian in space, her mission was more than just a personal dream—it was about inspiring millions of students and teachers across the world. She was ready for the challenge, trusting in the NASA engineers and the shuttle's reliability. She had no way of knowing about the conversations happening behind closed doors or the anomalies quietly registering on hidden screens.

In mission control, Flight Director Jay Greene gave the go-ahead. His team was laser-focused, their eyes glued to their monitors, listening to the rhythmic beeps of data pouring in. They had been briefed on the technical concerns, but in the final analysis, all systems were go. The shuttle was cleared for launch.

The countdown reached its final moments.

"T-minus ten... nine... eight..."

Around the world, millions of people watched the screen. Children cheered in classrooms, teachers held their breath, and families sat together in their living rooms, witnessing what they believed would be another great leap for humanity.

"Seven... six... five..."

On the ground at Cape Canaveral, the tension was palpable. The temperature remained cold, far colder than any previous launch. Icicles clung to the gantry, reflecting the brilliant morning sun. But the engines roared to life, and the ground shook with the force of their power.

"Four... three... two..."

In the hidden control room, Dr. Hayes and his team watched in silence as a final anomaly spiked on their monitors, stronger and more intense than anything they had recorded before. It flashed across their screens for a brief moment, then disappeared.

"What the hell is that?" someone muttered.

Hayes didn't answer. He couldn't. The shuttle had already begun its ascent.

"One... Liftoff!"

With a deafening roar, Challenger rose from the launch pad, climbing steadily into the sky. Flames shot from its engines as it pierced the cold, blue morning, trailing a plume of smoke behind it. Cheers erupted across the world. It was a moment of triumph, a symbol of humanity's unrelenting drive to explore the unknown.

But in the control rooms—both public and secret—the cheers were more reserved. For those who knew about the O-rings, the strange signals, and the anomalies, this was a moment fraught with tension. No one dared speak of their doubts now. The shuttle was airborne, and there was no turning back.

As Challenger climbed higher and higher, disappearing into the sky, the world watched in awe.

And then, 73 seconds into flight, everything changed.

Chapter 11: The First Signs

Inside the Challenger, moments before liftoff, everything seemed to be progressing as expected. The astronauts, strapped into their seats, went through their final checklists. The cockpit was filled with the familiar hum of machinery and the steady communication between the crew and mission control. Yet beneath the routine motions, something felt slightly... off.

Commander Francis R. Scobee kept his gaze forward, watching the instruments closely as they approached liftoff. His training had taught him to detect the smallest irregularities, but for now, everything appeared normal. Still, there was a faint sense of unease in the back of his mind—something he couldn't quite place.

Christa McAuliffe, sitting in her seat, was filled with excitement. She had been preparing for this day for months, and now, as the world watched, she felt a rush of adrenaline. But in the final minutes before liftoff, she, too, felt something unusual—a brief sensation of weightlessness, like the sudden drop of an elevator. It passed quickly, but it left her with an odd feeling in her stomach. She glanced at her fellow crew members, wondering if they had felt it too, but no one said anything.

As the countdown approached its final moments, the feeling returned, this time stronger. The shift in gravity was subtle but unmistakable. It wasn't like the anticipated weightlessness they'd soon experience in orbit. This was different—an odd, fluctuating pull that made their bodies feel light one moment and heavy the next, as if something was manipulating the very forces of gravity within the shuttle.

Pilot Michael J. Smith noticed it first. His hands hovered over the controls, and for a split second, he felt as though he was being lifted from his seat. Then, just as quickly, the sensation disappeared, leaving him momentarily disoriented.

"What the hell...?" he muttered under his breath, his mind racing to find an explanation.

In the seat next to him, Scobee noticed the brief look of confusion on Smith's face. He didn't ask, but he, too, had felt it—an odd shift, as though the shuttle's internal systems had momentarily malfunctioned. But everything on the control panel remained steady. He glanced at the altimeter, the gyros, and the gauges. There was no indication that anything was wrong. Yet, the feeling persisted, like a ghost in the cockpit, unsettling and unexplained.

"Mission control, this is Challenger," Scobee said, keeping his voice calm despite the strange sensation. "We're feeling a slight gravitational shift up here. You reading anything abnormal on your end?"

There was a brief pause before the familiar voice of Flight Director Jay Greene came over the comms. "Negative, Challenger. All readings look normal from here. Repeat, all systems are go."

Scobee exchanged a quick glance with Smith, both men silently acknowledging that something wasn't right, but neither willing to press the issue just yet. Time was running out, and the countdown continued.

In the back of the shuttle, Mission Specialist Ellison Onizuka also felt the strange pull. For a brief moment, he thought his seat restraints had loosened as he was tugged upward, but a quick check showed everything was secure. He frowned, trying to shake the disorientation. This wasn't like anything he had experienced in simulations, and yet, the instruments remained steady.

Judith Resnik, sitting next to Onizuka, felt her stomach lurch as the strange shift in gravity passed through the cabin again, like a wave rolling invisibly through the shuttle. She gripped her seat, trying to steady herself. There was no reason for this—it wasn't supposed to happen during pre-launch.

"Anyone else feel that?" she whispered, keeping her voice low.

Onizuka nodded slightly but said nothing. They were seconds away from liftoff, and it wasn't the time to start questioning the unknown. Still, the sense of unease gnawed at him.

The shift passed again, and this time, Christa McAuliffe winced. She wasn't used to the odd, fluctuating sensation. Her training had prepared her for the rigors of spaceflight, but no one had mentioned anything like this. She took a deep breath, focusing on the countdown and trying to push the unsettling feeling to the back of her mind.

As the final seconds counted down, the strange sensation of fluctuating gravity seemed to fade, replaced by the familiar, intense vibration of the shuttle's engines igniting. The roar was deafening, and within moments, Challenger lifted off the pad, climbing steadily into the sky. The momentary disorientation gave way to the familiar force of g-forces pressing them into their seats as the shuttle accelerated.

But for the astronauts, the memory of that brief, inexplicable shift in gravity lingered in the back of their minds. They had trained for every possible contingency, every imaginable scenario, but this—whatever it was—didn't fit into any known category.

As Challenger ascended, none of the crew members knew that down below, in NASA's classified monitoring rooms, scientists and engineers were also grappling with the unexplained. The strange, fluctuating gravitational anomalies weren't just a sensation within the shuttle—they were being detected on instruments both on the ground and in orbit. The data showed brief, localized distortions around the shuttle's immediate vicinity, as though something unseen was interfering with the gravitational field around the spacecraft.

In the hidden control room, Dr. Allan Hayes stood over a monitor, watching the data flash across the screen. The gravitational shifts were brief, but the pattern was unmistakable. His team had seen something similar during the earlier shuttle missions, but never this pronounced, never this close to the shuttle itself.

"What are we looking at?" one of his technicians asked, his voice filled with disbelief. "This doesn't make sense."

Dr. Hayes didn't respond immediately. He was staring at the anomaly, his mind racing. Could it be connected to the strange signals they had been tracking? Or was it something else entirely? Whatever it was, it defied explanation, but there was no time to dwell on it now.

"Log everything," Hayes ordered, his voice steady despite the growing unease in his gut. "We'll analyze it later."

As Challenger continued its ascent, the crew pushed the earlier disorientation to the back of their minds, focusing instead on their mission. But the strange gravitational shifts they had experienced before liftoff left an unsettling question unanswered—one that would soon resurface in ways they could never have imagined.

For now, the shuttle seemed stable, rising higher and higher, the world watching in awe. But beneath the surface of triumph, something unseen lurked, something that had made its presence known in those final moments before ascent.

And it wasn't finished yet.

Chapter 12: Into the Abyss

As the Challenger space shuttle thundered off the launch pad, the world watched in awe. The flames of its powerful engines ignited the cold Florida morning, and a massive plume of smoke and fire trailed behind as it climbed steadily into the clear blue sky. The roar of the engines drowned out everything for miles around, but for the seven astronauts on board, the noise was just another part of the familiar cacophony of launch. All systems were go, and from the outside, everything appeared flawless.

But behind the excitement of the global broadcast, in the quieter and more secretive corners of NASA, not everyone was convinced things were running smoothly.

In a hidden control room deep within Kennedy Space Center, where a small team monitored classified data from multiple sources, Dr. Allan Hayes kept his eyes fixed on a bank of monitors. His team had been tracking anomalies for days—strange signals, radar distortions, and unexplained readings that seemed to intensify as the Challenger's launch neared. Now, with the shuttle rocketing into space, Dr. Hayes and his team were on edge, waiting for any further signs of the unknown.

Just as Challenger passed through 40,000 feet, an alert flashed on one of the external monitoring screens. It was a brief flash of energy near the shuttle's trajectory—quick, too fast for the untrained eye to detect, but unmistakable on the instruments. A bright burst of light, almost imperceptible to the naked eye, appeared just beyond the shuttle's external camera feed. It was so fleeting that most in mission control didn't even notice it, but in the classified monitoring room, it sent a wave of unease through the team.

"What was that?" one of the technicians said, leaning closer to the monitor.

Dr. Hayes moved to his side, staring at the feed as the image replayed. The external camera, mounted to track the shuttle's ascent, had captured a split-second flash of light. It wasn't part of the shuttle's ignition, nor was it atmospheric reflection. It appeared out of nowhere, just a few hundred meters from the shuttle.

"Could be a lens flare," another technician suggested, though his voice lacked conviction. "Or maybe just a camera glitch."

But Dr. Hayes wasn't convinced. He had seen similar phenomena before, during other shuttle missions, though never this close to the spacecraft and never this strong. He replayed the footage, watching the burst of light in slow motion. It was too localized to be a flare, and the energy signature wasn't consistent with any known camera malfunction. It had appeared briefly, then vanished—just long enough to be captured, but too fast to be dismissed as ordinary interference.

"There's something more here," Hayes muttered, pulling up the energy readings from the shuttle's telemetry. "I don't think that was a glitch."

He cross-referenced the external data with readings from the shuttle's onboard systems. Just as the flash appeared, a spike registered in the shuttle's external temperature sensors—a spike too small to alert mission control but significant enough to show up in the data logs. It was as if the shuttle had passed through an invisible energy field, something beyond the understanding of traditional engineering.

Hayes hesitated, knowing that raising an alarm now would lead to questions he couldn't answer. The official narrative was set: the launch was going smoothly, the shuttle was functioning as expected, and the world was watching with admiration. There was no room for doubt.

"Could it be debris?" another technician asked, breaking the silence.

"No," Hayes replied, shaking his head. "Debris doesn't behave like this. And it's too close to the shuttle's flight path to be anything we've tracked."

As the team continued to analyze the data, the shuttle continued its ascent, moving toward the upper atmosphere. For the crew inside Challenger, everything seemed routine. The earlier disorientation caused by the inexplicable gravitational shifts had passed, replaced by the familiar press of g-forces as the shuttle climbed. Commander Scobee remained focused on the instruments, making minor adjustments as they ascended. He had momentarily dismissed the strange sensations before liftoff, attributing them to launch nerves or an unknown technical quirk. There was no time for distractions now.

Unbeknownst to Scobee and the rest of the crew, the brief flash of energy outside the shuttle was being quietly logged and monitored. Yet, despite Dr. Hayes' growing concern, the anomaly was officially dismissed as a camera glitch—a convenient explanation for something that had no clear answer.

In mission control, the atmosphere was one of quiet relief. So far, everything appeared normal. The launch had gone smoothly, the shuttle was on course, and the public was none the wiser to the tensions simmering beneath the surface. The engineers and flight directors kept their eyes on their monitors, listening to the steady stream of data flowing in from the shuttle's instruments.

But in the back of their minds, some of the more experienced engineers couldn't shake the feeling that something was off. The earlier warnings about the O-rings, the strange anomalies in the telemetry, and now, in the hidden corners of NASA, the unexplained energy readings—none of it made sense, and yet it was all happening in real-time.

In the hidden control room, Dr. Hayes leaned back in his chair, his eyes still locked on the screen. The energy spike hadn't returned, but the brief burst of light lingered in his mind. He knew better than to trust easy explanations, and the data didn't lie. Something had happened, something beyond their understanding, but with Challenger still climbing toward the edge of space, there was little he could do now but watch.

As the shuttle neared the crucial point of staging, where the solid rocket boosters would separate, Hayes' unease deepened. The external cameras showed nothing unusual, and mission control remained focused on the routine aspects of the flight. Yet Hayes knew that the burst of energy was no accident—it had appeared too suddenly, too close to the shuttle, and it had left behind a mark in the data.

But there was no time to dwell on it. The world was watching, and the Challenger's mission had become a symbol of hope, progress, and inspiration. To question that now, in the middle of the mission, would cause chaos. For now, the flash would be logged as a glitch, an anomaly with no immediate consequence.

And yet, as Challenger reached 73 seconds into its flight, Dr. Hayes could feel it—the growing tension, the invisible weight pressing down on him. Something was about to happen. He didn't know what, but the flash of energy wasn't the end. It was just the beginning.

And as the seconds ticked by, he braced for whatever came next.

Chapter 13: 73 Seconds

The Challenger's ascent had been, for the most part, a textbook launch. From the ground, it seemed flawless—an awe-inspiring symbol of human ingenuity, pushing through the cold Florida skies toward the heavens. The world watched with anticipation, unaware of the anomalies that had plagued the days leading up to this moment. For 73 seconds, the mission looked like it would be remembered for all the right reasons.

Then, in an instant, everything changed.

In Mission Control, the room was filled with the hum of machinery and quiet chatter. Engineers and flight directors monitored their screens, tracking the shuttle's progress, as their eyes darted between telemetry readouts and the live camera feed. Tension and excitement mixed as the Challenger passed through the critical stage of flight, where the solid rocket boosters would soon separate.

But just as the shuttle reached 73 seconds into flight, a sudden, violent explosion rocked the sky.

The world watched in stunned silence as the Challenger, once soaring triumphantly, was engulfed in a blinding flash of light. The shuttle seemed to disintegrate in midair, bursting apart in a chaos of smoke, debris, and fire, leaving behind an eerie, spiraling trail in the cold, blue sky.

In Mission Control, gasps filled the room as screens flashed red with warning signs. The data feed from the shuttle went dead, replaced by an avalanche of failure alerts. For a few agonizing moments, no one moved, no one spoke. The impossible had just happened. NASA's pride, their flawless space program, had turned to ash in front of the world.

But something even stranger was unfolding in those final milliseconds. Time, it seemed, had not followed its usual course.

For those watching on the ground, the explosion appeared instantaneous, the shuttle vanishing in the blink of an eye. But for a few, the experience was different—distorted, as if the event hadn't happened in real-time. Witnesses, including some in the control room and others watching from Cape Canaveral's launch site, later recalled seeing the explosion unfold in slow motion, as though time itself had warped.

Dr. Allan Hayes, still monitoring the classified data in his hidden control room, was one of the first to notice the anomaly. As the explosion rocked the Challenger, he was hit with an overwhelming sense of déjà vu—a surreal, gut-wrenching feeling that he had seen this event before, only this time it was happening out of sync. The explosion didn't just happen—it seemed to stretch, as if frozen in time for just a few moments longer than it should have. On his monitors, the data stream faltered and then appeared to stutter, showing a brief, inexplicable rewind before going completely black.

Hayes blinked in disbelief. Did he imagine it? The data stream, though lost, had glitched in a way that made no sense—flashes of readings that shouldn't exist, numbers that defied explanation. His team exchanged confused glances, but no one said a word. There was no protocol for what they had just witnessed.

The odd sensation wasn't confined to Hayes and his team. At Cape Canaveral, a group of onlookers—reporters, NASA staff, and families watching from the ground—would later describe seeing the explosion in eerie detail, each claiming that the event had unfolded in slow motion. Some said they saw the shuttle begin to break apart before the explosion, describing minute details that seemed impossible to perceive in real-time. Others swore that the shuttle had briefly flickered, as though it had "blinked" in and out of existence in the moments before the explosion.

Mission Specialist Judith Resnik, who had been seated in the middle of the shuttle's crew compartment, had a similar, disorienting experience. Just before the explosion, as Challenger roared toward space, she felt a strange shift—a brief moment where everything around her seemed to slow down. It was as if the shuttle had passed through something unseen, a distortion she couldn't explain. The other crew members were focused on their instruments, but Resnik couldn't shake the feeling that time had somehow stretched.

And then, it happened. A brilliant flash of light, followed by the deafening roar of destruction. She felt herself being thrown backward as the cabin violently buckled, and for the briefest second, her mind seemed to split. In that instant, she saw something—an image, a flash of light, a glimpse of... another place. It was impossible to describe, but in those final milliseconds, she swore she saw a vision of the shuttle intact, floating peacefully in space, far from the chaos of the explosion.

Commander Scobee, too, experienced a moment of temporal disorientation. In the instant before the explosion, his hands had hovered over the shuttle's controls, adjusting their trajectory. But as the explosion ripped through the shuttle, he experienced a strange sensation of time slowing down, just long enough to register what was happening in agonizing detail. He could see the glow of fire licking the edges of the cockpit, hear the groan of metal warping under intense pressure. It all happened in less than a second, but in his mind, it stretched out, as though time had given him a brief moment to understand the inevitable.

Back on the ground, in the silence that followed the explosion, confusion reigned. Mission Control was in chaos. Red lights flashed across every screen, showing nothing but error codes and warnings. Flight Director Jay Greene, his voice tight with shock, tried to regain control of the situation.

"We've had a major malfunction," Greene announced over the radio, his words hollow in the stunned silence of the control room.

As technicians scrambled to recover telemetry data, Dr. Hayes and his team quietly logged the final readings from the hidden control room. The energy spike they had detected earlier was back—brief, but massive. And more troublingly, it seemed to coincide precisely with the moment of the explosion, as though the two events were linked.

"Did anyone else see that?" one of Hayes' technicians whispered, his eyes wide with disbelief. "The explosion... it didn't happen normally. It was... slow."

Hayes nodded slowly, unable to explain what had just happened. The telemetry data was clear: something had interfered with the normal flow of time. He could see it in the logs, in the readings that showed brief, impossible jumps backward before cutting out entirely. And though there was no scientific explanation, he felt deep in his bones that the anomalies they had been tracking for weeks were somehow tied to this moment.

In the aftermath of the explosion, the world was left reeling. Grief and shock poured from every corner of the globe as news of the disaster spread. But amid the devastation, a few quiet voices whispered of strange things, of time warping, of glimpses of the shuttle as it once was, whole and undamaged. It was as though, in the final milliseconds of the Challenger's flight, the fabric of reality itself had twisted, and only a few had been able to perceive it.

For Dr. Hayes, the question remained: Had the strange energy signature, the one they had been tracking for so long, played a role in the disaster? Or had it simply provided a glimpse into something far more profound, something beyond human comprehension?

As the debris from the Challenger fell into the ocean, so too did the weight of the unanswered questions—a collision of time, space, and tragedy, with only fragments of truth left behind.

And so, the mystery deepened.

Chapter 14: Echoes of the Explosion

The sky above Cape Canaveral was a swirl of smoke, flame, and disbelief. In the immediate aftermath of the Challenger disaster, debris began to rain down from the heavens, a grim reminder of the catastrophic event that had unfolded just moments earlier. Pieces of the shuttle scattered across the ocean, some falling into the nearby marshlands, while others drifted down like ash over the stunned crowd below. The launch site was eerily quiet, save for the distant wail of emergency sirens and the soft cries of those who had come to witness history—only to see it torn apart in an instant.

NASA's mission control was frozen in shock. The silence in the room was deafening as engineers, flight directors, and technicians stared at their screens, trying to process what had just happened. The data feeds had gone black, replaced by emergency codes and failures across every system. For most, the event had been sudden and instantaneous—a tragic failure, an explosion. But for a few, there was something else. Something that didn't make sense.

As pieces of the Challenger continued to fall, strange data began to filter in from NASA's satellite network. High above Earth, a series of satellites tasked with monitoring the shuttle's trajectory had recorded the explosion—but not in the way anyone expected. Instead of capturing a straightforward event, the satellites had detected anomalies in both time and space, readings that hinted at something far more complicated than a simple mechanical failure.

In the classified control room where Dr. Allan Hayes and his team were stationed, the atmosphere was tense. They had watched the explosion unfold, just like everyone else, but what they were now seeing on their screens defied logic. The telemetry data, which had cut out at the moment of the explosion, was briefly replaced by a burst of energy readings that didn't align with any known physics. The readings showed two distinct events occurring in parallel—one, the explosion that the world had witnessed, and another, a phantom event that seemed to mirror the first but existed just outside their understanding.

"What are we looking at?" one of Hayes' technicians asked, his voice shaky.

Hayes leaned over the console, examining the data with a growing sense of dread. The satellite feeds showed something remarkable. For a split second—less than a fraction of a moment—there had been a double image of the shuttle. One version showed Challenger as it had been: whole, rising into space. The other showed the destruction, the debris scattering across the sky. It was as though the shuttle had existed in two states at once, one intact and one shattered.

"This isn't possible," Hayes muttered under his breath, his mind racing to find a rational explanation. But there wasn't one. The satellites had picked up readings of an alternate event—a timeline, perhaps, where the explosion hadn't occurred, where the Challenger had continued its ascent. And then, just as quickly as it had appeared, the anomaly disappeared, leaving only the grim reality of the disaster behind.

Another technician chimed in, staring at his screen in disbelief. "Look at the radiation levels. They spiked right before the explosion... and then again, just after. But here's the thing—there's no known source for this kind of radiation in Earth's orbit."

Hayes felt a chill run down his spine. The energy readings were unlike anything they had ever seen before. Whatever had caused the strange anomalies leading up to the Challenger launch was still present, lingering in the atmosphere like an echo. It was as if the explosion had torn a hole in reality itself, and for a brief moment, they were seeing not just the physical destruction of the shuttle, but an alternate possibility—an event that had happened, or almost happened, in another timeline.

He quickly pulled up the satellite data logs, hoping to make sense of what was unfolding. The readings didn't lie. For nearly a full second after the explosion, the satellite had captured images of a second Challenger, whole and unharmed, flying alongside the wreckage. The data showed overlapping energy signatures, suggesting that two versions of the shuttle had briefly existed in the same space.

Hayes turned to his team, his face pale. "We need to isolate this data and lock it down. This can't get out."

The technicians nodded, though their expressions were ones of fear and confusion. They were trained to deal with the unexpected, but this... this was something beyond the scope of any scientific knowledge. Time, space, and reality itself seemed to have warped around the Challenger in those final moments, leaving behind only fragments of what might have been.

Meanwhile, outside NASA's control rooms, debris continued to fall into the Atlantic, each piece a reminder of the lives lost. The media scrambled to cover the unfolding disaster, reporters struggling to find the right words as they narrated the shocking images for millions of viewers. Search and rescue teams were already being deployed to recover what they could, but there was little hope. The explosion had been too sudden, too devastating.

For those who had witnessed the event in real-time, it seemed clear: something had gone horribly wrong with the shuttle. But as the hours passed, a few individuals—astronauts, engineers, and bystanders—began to report seeing something strange. Some claimed they had seen a "double flash" in the sky, almost like a split in the air just before the explosion. Others swore they had seen the shuttle continue for a moment longer than it should have, hanging impossibly in the air before it was consumed by the blast.

These accounts, dismissed by most as shock or confusion in the aftermath of the tragedy, were quietly logged by NASA. They mirrored the strange readings coming in from the satellites, suggesting that for a brief moment, the Challenger had been caught in something far stranger than anyone could have imagined.

At NASA headquarters, the senior officials who had been briefed on the anomalies leading up to the launch now gathered in a tense, closed-door meeting. The telemetry glitches, the unexplained gravitational shifts, the energy spikes—none of it could be explained away any longer. Something had been happening around the Challenger, something that had interfered with the very fabric of reality.

Director Harold Duncan, one of the few who had been aware of the hidden concerns surrounding the mission, stood at the head of the table. His face was pale, his voice tight with barely contained anger and fear. "We need answers. Now."

But the answers weren't coming. Not yet.

In the classified room, Hayes continued to analyze the data, knowing full well what it could mean. The strange signals they had detected before the launch, the burst of energy during the explosion, and now these bizarre readings from the satellites—all pointed to one terrifying possibility: the Challenger disaster had somehow fractured time, leaving behind echoes of an alternate event that no one could fully understand.

As the cleanup efforts began and the world mourned the loss of the Challenger crew, Hayes and his team worked in silence, knowing that what they had witnessed—and what the data showed—would never be revealed to the public. Whatever had happened during those 73 seconds was far more than a simple mechanical failure. It was a glimpse into something much larger, something that defied human understanding.

And as the debris continued to fall from the sky, the echoes of the explosion lingered, haunting the few who had seen what lay beyond the veil of reality.

Chapter 15: The Disappearance

As the world reeled from the tragedy of the Challenger explosion, governments and agencies across the globe quickly began processing the data and preparing their public responses. News outlets carried the horrific images of the shuttle's mid-air disintegration, and NASA scrambled to manage the growing media frenzy. In the public eye, the narrative was clear: a catastrophic failure had occurred, resulting in the tragic loss of all seven astronauts.

But behind the veil of official statements, a far more perplexing story was unfolding—one that few outside of a select group of government officials and intelligence operatives would ever know.

Within hours of the explosion, classified reports began trickling into the hands of key government operatives—reports that contradicted the public narrative in chilling ways. These reports, sent from various military and intelligence agencies that had been quietly monitoring the launch for different reasons, contained data that was never meant to be seen by the public. Satellite images, classified telemetry logs, and confidential surveillance footage painted a picture far more complex—and far more disturbing—than a simple explosion.

At the heart of this mystery were the strange anomalies recorded at the moment of the Challenger's destruction. Several classified satellites positioned to monitor Earth's atmosphere and space had captured something unusual. While the explosion was undeniable, certain parts of the shuttle seemed to have... vanished entirely.

In one of the Pentagon's secure briefing rooms, high-ranking military officials and intelligence operatives sat in tense silence as the latest classified reports were reviewed. General Arthur Reese, a stern-faced man who had overseen numerous covert operations, stood at the front of the room, flipping through the classified documents on the podium. His face was unreadable, but the tension in the air was palpable. He cleared his throat before speaking.

"Gentlemen, what you're about to see stays in this room," Reese began, his voice firm. "Officially, the Challenger exploded. That's the story the world knows, and that's the story we're sticking with. But some of the data we've received suggests something else happened—something we can't explain."

He gestured to the technician seated by the projector. The lights dimmed, and a series of satellite images flashed onto the screen at the front of the room. The first few images showed the shuttle at the moment of the explosion, a massive fireball ripping through the fuselage and sending debris scattering in every direction.

But as the next image appeared, the room fell silent. The explosion was visible, but several key sections of the shuttle—the crew cabin, parts of the boosters—were simply gone. Not destroyed, not disintegrated—gone, as if they had been erased from existence.

"This was taken by a classified satellite monitoring high-orbit debris," Reese explained. "It captured the explosion, but notice here—there are missing sections of the shuttle. Not destroyed. Missing."

One of the men in the room, a CIA operative named Dan Foster, leaned forward, his brow furrowed. "What are you saying, General? That parts of the shuttle just... disappeared?"

Reese nodded. "That's exactly what I'm saying. This isn't just destruction. Something more is going on here. Whatever caused this... it didn't behave the way we expected."

The next image showed a brief flash of light, similar to the one Dr. Allan Hayes and his team had observed from their control room at NASA. It was a burst of energy, occurring just as the explosion happened. But here, in these classified images, it looked different—more concentrated, almost as if it had created a void where parts of the shuttle had once been.

Another official, a member of the Department of Defense's advanced surveillance team, spoke up. "We've run simulations, analyzed the telemetry, and cross-referenced everything we've got. There's no known weapon, no atmospheric condition, nothing in our database that can explain what we're seeing. It's like certain parts of the shuttle just ceased to exist."

The room was silent as the gravity of the situation settled in. The implications were staggering. For years, NASA had dealt with strange anomalies—unexplained signals, strange telemetry glitches—but nothing like this had ever happened. Now, the disaster was unfolding in ways no one could have anticipated.

General Reese continued, flipping to another classified report. "Here's where it gets even stranger. We've got reports from our deep-space monitoring stations—top-secret installations we use to track unidentified objects in orbit. They picked up something during the launch. At first, we thought it was debris. But whatever it was, it was moving too fast, and it wasn't following the normal trajectory."

The image on the screen shifted to a radar reading, showing an unidentified object appearing briefly near the shuttle's flight path just before the explosion. The object wasn't part of the shuttle, nor was it debris. It had appeared out of nowhere, hovered near the Challenger for a fraction of a second, and then vanished again—just as parts of the shuttle disappeared.

The implications were staggering. Was it possible that something—or someone—had interfered with the Challenger during its flight? And if so, what was the purpose of removing parts of the shuttle?

Dan Foster, the CIA operative, broke the silence. "Are we considering the possibility of... external interference? Something beyond our understanding?"

Reese met his gaze, his expression hard. "At this point, we have to consider every possibility. The radiation spikes, the gravitational anomalies before launch, and now this... whatever it is, it doesn't fit any known scientific explanation."

One of the military officials, a scientist specializing in space phenomena, leaned forward. "If parts of the shuttle disappeared, where did they go? Are we talking about some kind of time distortion? A rift?"

Reese exhaled deeply. "We don't know. But we do know this: certain sections of the shuttle, including the crew cabin, were never recovered. Not destroyed—just gone."

The room fell into an uneasy silence. These revelations went far beyond the official narrative being presented to the world. If parts of the shuttle had truly vanished—perhaps even been transported elsewhere—it opened up terrifying possibilities about what might have been involved in the disaster.

"What do we do with this information?" one of the intelligence officials asked.

"We bury it," Reese replied, his voice firm. "As far as the public is concerned, the Challenger exploded due to mechanical failure. We're not going to suggest anything beyond that. Not until we understand what we're dealing with."

The officials nodded in agreement, but the unease in the room was palpable. No one knew what to make of the data—what it meant, or what it suggested about the forces at play. But one thing was clear: the Challenger disaster was not just a tragedy. It was a mystery—one that reached far deeper than anyone had anticipated.

As the meeting concluded and the operatives filed out, General Reese remained behind, staring at the final image on the screen. The void where the shuttle had once been haunted him. Something had taken it—something beyond their understanding.

And as the debris continued to rain down into the ocean, so too did the unsettling knowledge that parts of the Challenger were no longer on Earth, nor anywhere that human science could explain.

Chapter 16: A Rift in Reality

Deep within NASA's labyrinthine research facilities, Dr. Eliza Langston sat hunched over a console, her fingers flying over the keyboard as she reviewed the latest batch of data from the Challenger mission. Unlike most of her colleagues, Eliza wasn't directly involved in the shuttle program itself. Her expertise lay in fringe physics, specifically in the study of anomalies in space-time. For years, her work had been relegated to the far reaches of theoretical science—interesting, but never considered critical to NASA's operations. That all changed when the Challenger exploded.

Eliza had been following the mission closely, not because she was directly involved, but because of the strange signals that had been reported in the days leading up to the launch. She had worked quietly, in the background, tracking the same anomalies that Dr. Allan Hayes and his team had detected, but with a different set of tools. And now, after hours of poring over the data, she was beginning to see something that chilled her to the core.

Her screen flashed with rows of telemetry data, interspersed with spikes in radiation and strange fluctuations in the shuttle's external readings. These were the same anomalies that had puzzled everyone at NASA—the gravitational shifts, the unexplained energy bursts—but as Eliza cross-referenced the data with her own research, a horrifying picture began to form.

Challenger hadn't just encountered a series of technical failures or unexplained energy spikes. It had passed through something far more profound.

Eliza paused for a moment, her breath catching in her throat. Could it really be what she thought it was? A dimensional rift? For years, her research had focused on the possibility of parallel dimensions and the theory that the fabric of space-time could be bent or even torn under certain conditions. But these had always been abstract ideas, confined to the realm of thought experiments and complex equations on a whiteboard. Now, though, she was looking at proof—proof that the Challenger had come into contact with a rift in reality itself.

She ran the data again, checking and rechecking the readings. The spikes in radiation and gravitational shifts weren't random—they formed a pattern. And that pattern aligned perfectly with the theory she had developed years ago, a theory about how the collision of certain energy fields in low Earth orbit could create a temporary tear in the fabric of space-time.

But it wasn't just a theory anymore. The data showed that Challenger had passed through one of these rifts, just seconds before the explosion.

Eliza's mind raced as she pieced together what must have happened. The strange energy spikes detected during the launch, the momentary fluctuations in gravity that the crew had felt—these were all signs that the shuttle had encountered a phenomenon far beyond NASA's understanding. And then, the explosion. Or rather, what everyone assumed had been an explosion.

The more Eliza studied the data, the more convinced she became that the explosion itself had been a byproduct of the rift. Challenger hadn't simply blown apart—it had been torn between two realities. For a brief moment, it had existed in two places at once: in our reality, where it had disintegrated, and in another, where the shuttle remained intact.

Her pulse quickened as she realized what this meant. The parts of the shuttle that had vanished weren't destroyed—they had been pulled into another dimension. The anomalies recorded by the satellites, the strange energy signatures, the reports of sections of the shuttle simply disappearing—everything pointed to the same conclusion.

She needed to tell someone, but who? This was classified information, and she wasn't even supposed to have access to some of these files. The risks were enormous, but Eliza knew she couldn't keep this to herself. The implications were too vast, too terrifying to ignore.

Eliza hastily compiled her findings into a report, encrypting it with multiple layers of security before sending it to Dr. Allan Hayes. He was the only one she trusted, and he had been tracking the same anomalies. If anyone would understand the gravity of what she had discovered, it was him.

As she waited for a response, Eliza continued to dig deeper into the data. She found more evidence—small but undeniable—that this was no ordinary explosion. A brief window of telemetry, recorded in the milliseconds before the disaster, showed the shuttle's velocity fluctuating in impossible ways, as though it were being pulled by forces not bound by the laws of physics.

And then there was the radiation spike. It had occurred precisely at the moment of the supposed explosion, a massive burst of energy unlike anything ever recorded during a shuttle launch. This wasn't a random event—it was the signature of a rift opening, a tear in the fabric of space-time itself.

Her phone buzzed, and she saw a message from Dr. Hayes: **"Meet me in Lab 17. Immediately."**

Eliza didn't hesitate. She grabbed her report and hurried through the maze of corridors, her heart pounding in her chest. Lab 17 was a secure facility, one of the few places within NASA where classified experiments were conducted. As she approached the lab, she swiped her ID card, and the door slid open with a soft hiss.

Inside, Dr. Hayes was waiting, his face pale and drawn. He had clearly been reviewing her report, and the look in his eyes confirmed what Eliza had already feared—he understood the implications all too well.

"You found it, didn't you?" Hayes said quietly, gesturing to the screen where her data was displayed.

Eliza nodded. "I think the Challenger passed through a dimensional rift. The energy spikes, the gravitational shifts, the disappearance of parts of the shuttle—it all fits. This wasn't just an explosion. Something tore the shuttle apart, but not in the way we thought."

Hayes ran a hand through his hair, his eyes wide with disbelief. "I've seen the same data, but I couldn't put it together until now. The explosion... it's almost like it didn't happen in real-time. We've got reports from witnesses saying they saw the shuttle in two places at once, just before it blew apart."

Eliza stepped forward, pulling up a model of the event on the lab's holographic display. "Exactly. It's as if the shuttle was straddling two realities—one where it continued its ascent, and one where it exploded. For a brief moment, both existed simultaneously."

Hayes stared at the display, his mind reeling. "So the missing sections of the shuttle—they didn't just vanish?"

"No," Eliza said, her voice barely above a whisper. "They were pulled into another dimension."

The enormity of the discovery hung in the air between them. If they were right, then the Challenger disaster was more than just a mechanical failure—it was the first known instance of a human-made object encountering a rift in reality. The implications were staggering. What else had been affected by this rift? Could the crew have survived in some alternate reality? What had caused the rift in the first place?

As they stood in silence, contemplating the impossible, Eliza knew one thing for certain: nothing about the Challenger disaster was as it seemed. They were standing on the edge of a new frontier, one where the laws of physics, time, and space themselves were no longer fixed.

And they had only just begun to understand the consequences.

Chapter 17: The Alternate Mission

In another version of reality, one no one on Earth could have possibly imagined, the Challenger continued its ascent smoothly through the crisp January sky. There was no explosion, no blinding flash of light, no debris raining down over the Atlantic. The shuttle's engines roared as expected, pushing the spacecraft higher and higher, and inside the crew compartment, the astronauts felt a sense of triumph as they broke free from the pull of Earth's gravity.

Commander Francis Scobee, seated at the controls, glanced at his instruments and saw nothing unusual. All systems were functioning perfectly. Christa McAuliffe smiled beneath her helmet, feeling the thrill of weightlessness for the first time. Everything was going according to plan—or so it seemed.

But while the Challenger in this timeline had escaped the catastrophic fate that befell it in another, something else had gone terribly wrong. The crew couldn't know it yet, but the moment their shuttle passed through a patch of space just beyond the atmosphere, something subtle, but profoundly disturbing, began to unfold.

At first, the shift was imperceptible. The Challenger sailed smoothly into orbit, and Scobee, with the assistance of Pilot Michael J. Smith, prepared the shuttle for the deployment of the communication satellite aboard. Everything seemed routine. However, within minutes of achieving orbit, strange glitches began appearing on the shuttle's displays.

"We're getting some weird readings here," Smith said, frowning at the control panel. "Temperature fluctuations, minor system errors, but nothing critical."

"Run diagnostics," Scobee ordered. He wasn't too concerned—glitches happened all the time in space, and their training had prepared them to handle just about anything. But something in the back of his mind tugged at him, a sense that these anomalies weren't just ordinary system quirks.

As Smith worked on recalibrating the instruments, the rest of the crew busied themselves with their respective tasks. Mission Specialist Judith Resnik was preparing the satellite deployment systems while McAuliffe rehearsed the lesson plans she would deliver to classrooms around the world from space. Mission Specialists Ronald McNair and Ellison Onizuka worked on their scientific experiments, reviewing their checklists and getting ready for the hours ahead. Everything felt as routine as space travel could be.

Then, something strange happened. The temperature inside the cabin began to drop—noticeably.

"Is it me, or is it getting colder in here?" McNair asked, rubbing his arms through the thick suit. "This isn't supposed to happen."

Scobee glanced at the environmental controls. The cabin temperature had dropped by nearly ten degrees in the span of a few minutes, and it was still falling.

"We're losing heat," Resnik said, her voice tinged with concern. "It's like the environmental systems are malfunctioning, but everything reads normal."

Scobee's fingers flew across the controls as he tried to bring the temperature back up, but nothing worked. The cabin grew colder still, and soon the astronauts could see their breath fogging in the air, despite their sealed suits.

"This doesn't make sense," Smith muttered, staring at the environmental systems readout. "The systems are running at full capacity, but it's like the heat is just... disappearing."

In the mission control room, far below on Earth, there were no immediate signs of trouble. The Challenger's telemetry showed minor anomalies, but nothing that would raise red flags. To the ground crew, the mission appeared to be running smoothly, with no indication that anything was wrong. The astronauts' communications with mission control remained normal, and there were no outward signs of malfunction.

But the crew aboard the Challenger was beginning to sense that something was deeply wrong—something that had nothing to do with the shuttle's mechanics.

As the minutes passed, the temperature continued to plummet, and strange phenomena began to unfold within the cabin. Resnik noticed it first—a subtle distortion in the air, almost like a shimmer, as if the space inside the shuttle was warping in strange ways. She blinked, convinced it was a trick of the light, but the effect didn't go away. The walls of the shuttle seemed to bend ever so slightly, warping at the edges of her vision before returning to normal.

"Do you see that?" she asked, her voice low and unnerved.

"See what?" McAuliffe replied, her attention still on her lesson plans.

Resnik hesitated. "The walls... they're moving. Just for a second, it's like everything is stretching and shrinking."

McAuliffe looked around, frowning, but everything appeared normal to her. "I don't see anything."

The crew continued their work, but the sense of unease grew. Soon, others began to notice it too—the strange distortions, the way the cabin felt like it was expanding and contracting ever so slightly. It was as if space itself was behaving unnaturally around them, as though they had drifted into a part of the cosmos where the laws of physics no longer applied.

Scobee was the next to notice something disturbing. The Earth, visible through the shuttle's front window, looked... wrong. He couldn't place it at first, but as they orbited the planet, the continents seemed slightly off. The familiar shape of North America was distorted, elongated in a way that defied explanation.

"What is that?" Scobee muttered, staring out at the Earth below. "The planet... it doesn't look right."

Smith looked over his shoulder, his eyes narrowing as he took in the sight. "That's impossible. The telemetry shows we're in the correct orbit."

But as the shuttle circled the Earth, the distortions became more apparent. Time itself seemed to shift, stretching and compressing in ways that made no sense. Instruments that should have been calibrated perfectly began to fail—clocks lost time, while others sped up. The crew reported flashes of strange visions—fleeting glimpses of another place, another reality, where the shuttle existed differently, where the mission had taken a different path.

Resnik's breath caught in her throat as a wave of vertigo swept over her. For a brief moment, she saw the shuttle not as it was, but as it might have been—an alternate timeline where Challenger had exploded, the debris scattering through the sky. She blinked, shaking her head, and the vision was gone.

"What's happening to us?" Onizuka whispered, his voice barely audible through the helmet's intercom.

"I don't know," Scobee replied, his own unease growing. "But we need to figure it out fast."

As the distortions worsened, the crew began to experience something even more terrifying: moments of disconnection. One by one, the astronauts felt as though they were slipping out of sync with the shuttle itself. It was as if, for brief moments, they no longer existed in the same place. McNair reached for a tool, only to find his hand passing through it, as though it wasn't solid. Resnik found herself unable to speak for several seconds, as if time had frozen just for her, while the others moved normally.

"Mission control, do you copy?" Scobee called out, trying to maintain his composure. "We're experiencing... anomalies. I don't know how to describe it. It's like we're not all here."

But mission control had no answer. From their perspective, everything appeared normal. The crew's voices came through clearly, and the telemetry, while showing minor fluctuations, gave no indication of the nightmare unfolding aboard the shuttle.

The Challenger continued to orbit, trapped between two realities—one where the mission had succeeded, and another where it had met with disaster. And as the hours wore on, the crew realized with growing dread that they were no longer in control of their fate. Something else had taken hold, something that defied explanation.

Scobee's hands shook as he gripped the controls, staring at the warped image of the Earth below. "We need to find a way out of this," he whispered, though he wasn't sure if anyone could hear him. "Before it's too late."

But even as he spoke, the sense of disconnection deepened. Time stretched, space warped, and the crew of the Challenger realized that they were no longer part of the world they knew. They had slipped into an alternate reality—one where their mission hadn't ended in an explosion, but in something far stranger, and far more dangerous.

And in the silence of space, they drifted further into the unknown, with no way of knowing if they would ever return.

Chapter 18: Whispers of the Phantom Shuttle

The Challenger disaster sent shockwaves through the world. In the days that followed, the nation mourned the loss of the seven astronauts who had perished in the explosion. Tributes poured in from every corner of the globe, and NASA was thrust into a period of intense scrutiny. Investigations were launched to determine what had gone wrong, but amidst the official reports and public condolences, whispers of something far stranger began to circulate.

At first, the rumors seemed like the usual fringe conspiracy theories that often emerge in the wake of tragedy. But as more details leaked from behind closed doors, the whispers became harder to dismiss. It wasn't just that the Challenger had exploded—some claimed it hadn't been destroyed at all. Instead, they said, the shuttle had been transported to another dimension, its crew caught between worlds, their fates unknown.

It began quietly, on obscure forums and in private conversations between engineers and insiders who had been close to the mission. Some had noticed anomalies in the data—anomalies that weren't publicly explained. Others pointed to the strange, brief flashes of light seen just before the explosion, or the unexplained telemetry spikes that seemed to suggest the shuttle had existed in two places at once. Then there were the classified satellite images, showing parts of the shuttle simply vanishing rather than being destroyed.

To those in the know, it was becoming clear that something about the Challenger disaster didn't add up. And while the official story focused on mechanical failure and tragic oversight, a different theory was quietly gaining momentum: the Challenger hadn't exploded—it had slipped into another dimension.

At the center of these rumors was a small group of engineers and scientists, many of whom had worked closely with NASA during the lead-up to the launch. Some had been present during the classified briefings where anomalies were discussed, and others had seen the strange satellite data with their own eyes. These individuals formed the backbone of a secret investigation, quietly conducted outside of the public's view.

One of these investigators was Dr. Allan Hayes. He had been among the first to notice the strange energy signatures and gravitational distortions leading up to the launch, and his team had been tracking the unusual signals long before the Challenger left the ground. But what he had discovered in the aftermath of the disaster shook him to his core. The data didn't just point to a mechanical failure—it hinted at something far more disturbing.

In the privacy of his small office, buried deep within NASA's research facility, Hayes reviewed the satellite logs again. The brief flash of light that appeared just before the explosion had been dismissed as a camera glitch by most, but to Hayes, it was a sign of something far more significant. The radiation spikes, the strange energy bursts, the fact that parts of the shuttle had seemed to vanish rather than be obliterated—it all pointed to a dimensional event, something that had torn the Challenger from reality.

The idea of a dimensional rift wasn't entirely new. Fringe scientists had theorized for decades that under certain conditions, the fabric of space-time could be warped, leading to the possibility of alternate realities. But these ideas had always been theoretical—until now.

Hayes leaned back in his chair, staring at the data. If the Challenger had indeed been pulled into another dimension, where was it now? And more importantly, could the crew still be alive? He couldn't shake the feeling that they were out there, somewhere—lost in a world that wasn't their own, trapped in a space between realities.

The conspiracy theories were growing, fueled by leaks and whispered conversations among those who had access to classified information. On the surface, the theories seemed wild—impossible, even. But for those who had seen the data, it was becoming harder to deny the possibility.

The idea of the "Phantom Shuttle," as it came to be known, began to take root. Some claimed that the shuttle had been caught in a temporal distortion, a rift that had transported it to another time or dimension just before the explosion. Others speculated that the energy burst seen in the satellite footage was the result of an experiment gone wrong, something NASA had been working on in secret.

In the darker corners of the conspiracy community, the theories became more outlandish. Some claimed that the Challenger crew had been part of a covert mission, one designed to explore the boundaries of space-time. They argued that NASA had known about the possibility of a dimensional rift all along, and that the shuttle's explosion had been a cover-up for the true nature of the mission.

Most dismissed these ideas as fantasy, but as more insiders began to speak out, the whispers grew louder. And as Hayes continued his investigation, he uncovered even more troubling evidence. Among the classified files he accessed were reports of previous anomalies during other shuttle missions—brief, unexplained glitches in telemetry, strange energy signatures, and sightings of what some described as "shadows" following the shuttles in low Earth orbit.

There was one report, in particular, that caught his attention: a shuttle mission from two years earlier, during which the crew had experienced unexplained gravitational shifts, much like those reported by the Challenger crew moments before the disaster. The telemetry data from that mission showed a similar pattern—an energy burst followed by a brief, unexplainable loss of signal. But unlike the Challenger, that shuttle had returned safely, and the incident had been quietly swept under the rug.

As Hayes dug deeper, he realized that the Challenger disaster might have been the culmination of years of unexplained phenomena. NASA had known about the anomalies, but no one had ever expected anything like this. The question that haunted him now was whether the rift had been a natural occurrence—or something triggered by human intervention.

Hayes wasn't the only one investigating the possibility of the Phantom Shuttle. In secret, a small team of government operatives had been tasked with uncovering the truth. Working under the radar, they sought out anyone who had access to the classified data, interviewing engineers, scientists, and satellite technicians who had been close to the mission. Their job was simple: find out what really happened to the Challenger, and, if possible, locate the shuttle.

One of the operatives, a man named Mark Whittaker, had spent years working in intelligence. He wasn't a scientist, but he knew how to find answers—and more importantly, how to keep secrets. As he interviewed those closest to the disaster, he began to piece together a picture that was far more complex than anything he had imagined. The classified reports, the strange readings, the anomalies—it all pointed to something beyond the scope of current science.

Whittaker's investigation led him to Hayes, and the two quickly realized they were on the same path. Together, they began to dig deeper, searching for any evidence that might explain what had happened to the Challenger. But as they worked, they were met with resistance. Key documents had been redacted, witnesses suddenly refused to speak, and some of the most crucial data had mysteriously disappeared from NASA's archives.

It became clear that someone—somewhere—was trying to bury the truth.

Despite the obstacles, Hayes and Whittaker pressed on. They knew they were close to something monumental, something that could change the way humanity understood the universe. The Challenger, they believed, wasn't gone—it was out there, in a place no one had ever explored. And the crew, lost between dimensions, might still be alive, waiting for rescue.

As the whispers of the Phantom Shuttle continued to spread, the secret investigation gained momentum. But with each step forward, the dangers grew. Powerful forces were at work, determined to keep the truth hidden. And as Hayes and Whittaker closed in on their answers, they began to realize that finding the Challenger might be the least of their worries.

The real question wasn't where the shuttle had gone—but what else might have come through the rift with it.

Chapter 19: The Fractured Sky

Weeks had passed since the Challenger disaster, and while the world was still grappling with the loss of the crew and the tragic failure of the mission, something else—something far stranger—was quietly unfolding. The anomaly that had torn through the sky on January 28, 1986, was beginning to leave its mark in unexpected ways. Across the globe, subtle yet disturbing changes were being detected, and the ripple effects were growing more apparent by the day.

It started with the weather.

Meteorologists were the first to notice the shifts. Unusual and erratic weather patterns began forming, seemingly out of nowhere. Storm systems that should have been predictable were behaving erratically, their paths twisting and distorting in ways that defied conventional forecasting models. Hurricanes formed far earlier in the season than expected, and their trajectories were more unpredictable than ever before, bending in ways that confounded experts.

Across the Midwest, a massive cold front settled over the region, plunging temperatures far below normal. In Europe, a heatwave scorched the continent, setting records in the dead of winter. And over the Atlantic Ocean, where the Challenger had met its tragic fate, strange atmospheric anomalies began to emerge. Pilots flying over the area reported turbulence unlike anything they had experienced before, and instruments aboard commercial jets recorded sudden shifts in air pressure, as if something invisible was distorting the atmosphere.

Satellite imagery of the Earth's weather patterns showed strange formations—circles and spirals of clouds that appeared without warning, then vanished just as quickly. What was even more disturbing was that these anomalies seemed to be concentrated in the very area where Challenger had exploded, rippling outward as if the disaster had left a tear in the sky itself.

Within NASA, a small group of scientists had begun to track these anomalies, though they were hesitant to draw any public conclusions. Dr. Eliza Langston, now one of the few who understood the true scope of what had happened, was at the center of this research. She had long suspected that the Challenger disaster had been more than just a tragic accident, and now the data seemed to confirm it.

"We're seeing distortions in the atmosphere," Eliza said during a private meeting with Dr. Allan Hayes and Mark Whittaker, the intelligence operative who had joined their investigation. They were gathered in a secure briefing room, far from prying eyes. "Weather patterns are being affected. It's as if something is disrupting the normal flow of energy through the Earth's atmosphere."

Hayes frowned as he reviewed the satellite data, noting the strange formations appearing across the globe. "It's not just weather, either," he said. "Satellite communication is being disrupted as well. We've had reports of signal blackouts, GPS malfunctions, and even strange bursts of radiation in low Earth orbit."

Whittaker leaned forward, his expression dark. "Are you saying this is all connected to the Challenger?"

Eliza hesitated for a moment before responding. "Yes. I think the anomaly left behind by the disaster is still active. The rift—if that's what it was—didn't just affect the shuttle. It's affecting the planet."

The thought was staggering, but the evidence was mounting. Since the day of the Challenger disaster, there had been a steady increase in atmospheric and electromagnetic disturbances. Radio signals were being distorted, and entire regions were experiencing unexplained power surges and outages. Military satellites, usually impervious to such issues, had reported strange glitches in their systems. And then there were the unusual radiation spikes, which seemed to align with the same type of energy signature detected during the Challenger's final moments.

"The rift," Hayes repeated quietly, as if testing the word. "If that's what we're dealing with, then we're looking at a tear in the fabric of space-time itself."

Whittaker's face tightened. "And it's not just theoretical anymore. This thing is real, and it's starting to have tangible effects on the world."

Eliza pulled up a map of the Earth on the room's large screen, overlaying it with satellite data. Red and orange clusters began to appear, marking the areas where the anomalies were most pronounced. The epicenter of the disturbances was clear: the Atlantic Ocean, directly over the area where the Challenger had disintegrated.

"What we're seeing is consistent with the idea that the explosion didn't just destroy the shuttle," Eliza explained. "It opened something. A rift, or a tear, in the sky. And now that tear is destabilizing the atmosphere around it."

The map showed the disturbances radiating outward from the epicenter, spreading across the globe like the ripples of a stone dropped in a pond. But these ripples weren't just affecting the weather. Communication satellites, critical to global infrastructure, were being hit hardest. Entire networks experienced outages and malfunctions, and GPS signals, which relied on precise timing and coordination, began to fail intermittently. For the global economy, these disruptions were dangerous—planes were forced to reroute, shipping lanes became unreliable, and financial markets saw brief, inexplicable flashes of chaos.

The strange occurrences weren't limited to the skies, either. On the ground, people began to report unusual phenomena. In small towns near Cape Canaveral, residents spoke of sudden changes in temperature, strange electrical surges, and even moments of disorientation. Some claimed they had seen brief flashes of light in the sky—pulses of energy that left the air humming with a strange, unsettling charge.

And then there were the whispers of something even more disturbing: objects vanishing without explanation. In the weeks after the Challenger disaster, a handful of incidents were reported where small objects—keys, tools, even entire cars—had disappeared, only to reappear minutes or hours later in completely different locations. The incidents were dismissed by most as the product of shock or trauma, but those tracking the Challenger anomaly couldn't ignore the pattern.

"What we're dealing with," Eliza said carefully, "might be more than just a rift in the atmosphere. The tear could be affecting the very fabric of reality. Space and time are being bent, distorted. And if that's the case, then we're looking at a much bigger problem."

Hayes rubbed his temples, the weight of the situation pressing down on him. "So what are we supposed to do? This is far beyond anything NASA or any government agency is equipped to handle."

"I don't know," Eliza admitted. "But we need to start monitoring these phenomena more closely. If this rift continues to destabilize, it could lead to something catastrophic."

Whittaker, who had remained silent for most of the conversation, finally spoke. "If word of this gets out, there'll be mass panic. We need to contain this, control the narrative before the world finds out what's really happening."

Hayes nodded. "Agreed. But we can't just sit on this. We need to figure out how to close the rift."

"That's assuming we even know what opened it in the first place," Eliza added grimly. "And that's the part that still doesn't make sense. The explosion shouldn't have caused this. Something else must have triggered it."

As the trio sat in the dimly lit room, grappling with the enormity of the problem, the skies above continued to fracture. The ripple effects of the anomaly were growing stronger by the day, and across the globe, scientists and engineers struggled to explain the unexplainable. Weather patterns shifted, satellites faltered, and the whispers of objects disappearing began to spread.

The Challenger disaster had opened something far beyond the physical realm. And now, the very fabric of reality was at risk of unraveling.

The fractured sky was only the beginning.

Chapter 20: The Investigation Begins

In the wake of the Challenger disaster, NASA and the U.S. government launched an immediate and highly public investigation to determine the cause of the explosion. The Rogers Commission, headed by former Secretary of State William P. Rogers, was established to lead the inquiry. Comprised of engineers, astronauts, and military officials, the commission's mandate was clear: to uncover the technical failures that led to the tragic loss of the shuttle and its crew.

The public followed every development closely, as news outlets reported on the mechanical failures, particularly focusing on the O-rings that had malfunctioned in the freezing temperatures. It was a straightforward narrative of human error, a tragic but comprehensible failure that resulted from avoidable circumstances. The media, the public, and even most of NASA's staff believed that this investigation would ultimately provide closure.

But beneath the surface, far from the public eye, a much deeper and more secretive investigation was quietly underway.

In a secure location, known only to a select few government officials and top-level NASA personnel, a classified inquiry had begun. This investigation wasn't concerned with the failure of the O-rings or the cold weather conditions. Instead, it focused on the anomalies that had been detected leading up to the launch, the strange energy spikes, the unexplainable telemetry glitches, and the bizarre weather patterns that had formed after the explosion.

Dr. Allan Hayes, already deeply involved in tracking these anomalies, had been unofficially appointed to lead the inquiry. His work, along with that of Dr. Eliza Langston and intelligence operative Mark Whittaker, had revealed troubling evidence that the Challenger disaster was more than just a mechanical failure. The rift—the tear in reality that had seemingly opened during the explosion—was their primary focus. But even as they dug deeper, they knew they were operating in the shadows. The official investigation couldn't be tainted by their findings, not yet.

At NASA headquarters, the mood was somber but determined. The Rogers Commission held public hearings, interviewing engineers, astronauts, and officials about the events leading up to the launch. Mortality statistics, risk assessments, and detailed breakdowns of the shuttle's design were presented. The failure of the O-rings was the leading theory, and all attention was directed toward the technical aspects of the shuttle's catastrophic failure.

Behind the scenes, however, Hayes and his team were following a different path.

They had been granted access to the highest levels of classified data—satellite readings, telemetry logs, and intelligence reports that had never been made public. These files contained the anomalies Hayes had been tracking since the days before the disaster, and they painted a far more disturbing picture. They showed that the energy spikes and gravitational distortions recorded during the Challenger's ascent were unlike anything NASA had ever seen.

In a small, secure room deep within NASA's research complex, Hayes, Eliza, and Whittaker gathered again, reviewing the latest data.

"Officially, the focus is still on the O-rings," Whittaker said, glancing at the pile of reports on the table. "But that's not going to explain what we're seeing here. The explosion wasn't just mechanical—something else triggered it."

Eliza nodded, her eyes scanning a printout of the radiation spikes recorded just before and after the explosion. "These energy readings don't make sense in the context of a standard shuttle launch. This isn't just a malfunction. The rift, or whatever it is, was already forming before the explosion occurred."

They had compiled a mountain of evidence, much of it classified. The satellite images of the burst of light just before the explosion, the reports of the shuttle seeming to exist in two places at once, and the strange electromagnetic disruptions in the atmosphere were all part of a pattern. The more they investigated, the more convinced they became that the Challenger had encountered something far beyond the scope of human understanding.

But as their investigation progressed, they began to encounter resistance. Critical data was suddenly classified even higher, access to certain files was restricted, and some of their requests for information were quietly denied. It was clear that someone—whether within NASA or elsewhere—was trying to keep their inquiry from advancing too far.

"What's happening?" Eliza asked one day, after yet another request for telemetry logs had been stonewalled. "We're hitting a wall everywhere we turn."

Hayes frowned, glancing at Whittaker. "Someone's shutting us down."

Whittaker, who had years of experience in intelligence, had suspected this might happen. The deeper they delved into the anomaly, the more dangerous their findings became—not just for NASA, but for the government itself. The implications of their work were staggering. If the Challenger had truly encountered a dimensional rift, if the explosion had torn a hole in reality, then the entire nature of the disaster would be redefined. It wouldn't be a simple case of technical failure; it would be evidence that humanity had stumbled upon forces it was not prepared to understand.

"We're dealing with something they can't let the public know about," Whittaker said, his voice low. "If this rift is real, and it's still open, we're talking about a threat to national security. They're not going to let us keep digging."

The team faced an impossible dilemma. Their investigation had revealed evidence of a world-altering event, but every move they made was being quietly monitored and obstructed. If they pushed too hard, they risked not only their careers but their safety. Yet the consequences of doing nothing were equally terrifying.

"We can't stop now," Eliza said, her voice resolute. "We've come too far. We need to know what really happened—and if the rift is still open, we need to find a way to close it."

Hayes nodded. "Agreed. But we're going to have to be careful. From here on out, we're operating outside the official investigation."

Whittaker stood, his expression grim. "I'll keep digging on my end. We've got people in the intelligence community who are asking the same questions. They know something's not right, even if they're not saying it outright."

As the days passed, the tension within NASA grew. The Rogers Commission pressed forward with its official investigation, preparing its final report on the Challenger disaster. But behind closed doors, Hayes, Eliza, and Whittaker continued their secret inquiry, gathering evidence, chasing leads, and monitoring the anomalies that seemed to be growing stronger by the day.

One evening, while reviewing satellite data in the privacy of his office, Hayes stumbled upon something that made his blood run cold. A set of encrypted files, buried deep within NASA's classified network, contained reports of a previous incident—an event that bore eerie similarities to what had happened with the Challenger.

It had occurred during a test flight years earlier, in the early days of the space shuttle program. The telemetry had shown unexplained energy spikes and gravitational distortions, much like the ones seen during Challenger's launch. The flight had been cut short, but the data had been quietly sealed away, labeled as a "technical anomaly" and never spoken of again.

Hayes' heart pounded as he realized the truth. The Challenger disaster wasn't the first time NASA had encountered this anomaly. It had been there all along, lurking in the background, waiting to strike again.

He quickly gathered his notes and called Eliza and Whittaker. They needed to see this. The deeper truth about the Challenger disaster was beginning to emerge, and it was more terrifying than they had ever imagined.

The rift wasn't an isolated event. It was part of a larger, more dangerous phenomenon—one that had been quietly hidden for years. And now, with the world still focused on the official investigation, Hayes knew they had to act quickly.

Because whatever had caused the Challenger to tear through reality wasn't finished yet. The investigation had only just begun.

Chapter 21: Fragments of the Future

The survivors of the Challenger program—those who had worked on the mission, the engineers, support staff, and even family members of the lost astronauts—had long struggled with the emotional weight of the disaster. For weeks after the explosion, they mourned, replayed the events in their minds, and tried to find closure as the official investigation unfolded. But as time passed, some began experiencing something far stranger than grief.

It started with dreams. Vivid, haunting dreams that felt more like memories than mere imagination. The survivors would wake, drenched in sweat, convinced they had witnessed something real. In their dreams, the Challenger hadn't exploded at all. Instead, they saw the shuttle soaring into space, the mission going forward as planned. In some dreams, the astronauts lived—returning heroes, their mission completed. But in others, the shuttle seemed to drift into something unknowable, its fate hanging in a suspended state between success and disaster.

At first, these visions were dismissed as a manifestation of trauma, the mind struggling to cope with the magnitude of the event. But for some, the dreams began to bleed into their waking life, leaving them with a persistent feeling that something was deeply wrong. They were living in one reality, but glimpsing another, one where the Challenger had not been lost.

One such survivor was Roger Boisjoly, the engineer whose warnings about the O-rings had gone unheard in the lead-up to the disaster. Wracked with guilt and anger after the explosion, he had struggled to move forward. But recently, Roger had begun to experience strange flashes of memory—memories that didn't belong to him. In these moments, he saw the Challenger not as a tragic failure, but as a successful mission, its crew alive and well. The flashes came at random: while he was driving, while he was reading, or even in the middle of the night as he lay awake, unable to sleep.

It wasn't just Roger, either. June Scobee Rodgers, widow of Commander Francis Scobee, had also begun experiencing inexplicable moments of déjà vu. In the weeks following the explosion, she had accepted the reality of her husband's death, but recently, she'd been struck by flashes of an alternate life. In this life, Francis had survived. She remembered embracing him when he returned from space, remembered the celebration of his successful mission. At first, she had chalked it up to grief playing tricks on her mind. But the memories felt too real, too specific. They weren't dreams—they were fragments of another existence.

As the visions became more frequent, those who experienced them began to question their own reality. Were these memories simply coping mechanisms, the brain's desperate attempt to rewrite history? Or were they something else—glimpses of an alternate timeline, one where the Challenger's fate had unfolded differently?

Dr. Allan Hayes had begun hearing rumors of these strange experiences through the hidden channels of his ongoing investigation. Some of the engineers and scientists who had worked on the Challenger program had contacted him privately, describing similar visions. It was too widespread to ignore, and as Hayes dug deeper, he found that those experiencing the phenomena were often the same individuals who had been closest to the anomalies leading up to the disaster.

One afternoon, as Hayes reviewed the latest reports in his office, his phone rang. It was Eliza Langston.

"Allan, we need to meet," she said, her voice tense. "There's something happening. People are reporting strange... visions. I've had three more engineers reach out to me today alone, all describing the same thing. They're seeing alternate realities—futures that never happened."

Hayes felt a chill run down his spine. "I've been hearing about it too. I think it's connected to the rift."

They met that evening in a secure room at NASA, along with Mark Whittaker, who had been quietly tracking the reports as well. Whittaker had connections within the intelligence community, and even some of his contacts had begun to notice the strange phenomenon. Government officials, military personnel, and even a few astronauts who hadn't been involved in the Challenger mission were starting to experience these disjointed visions.

"It's like pieces of an alternate timeline are bleeding through into ours," Eliza said, pacing the room as she spoke. "The people who are having these visions aren't just remembering different futures—they're seeing them. They're catching glimpses of what could have been. And it's spreading."

Hayes leaned forward, his brow furrowed. "The rift. It must have fractured the timeline. The Challenger wasn't just caught in a physical anomaly—it was torn between realities. And now, those realities are overlapping."

Whittaker remained quiet, his eyes scanning the reports they had compiled. "We need to keep this contained. If this gets out, there'll be chaos. People are already questioning the official narrative, but if they find out the timeline itself might have been altered..."

"What if we're wrong?" Eliza asked. "What if the Challenger didn't just explode? What if it's still out there, in some other dimension? What if these visions are fragments of the future that could have happened—or maybe still is happening somewhere else?"

The idea hung heavy in the air. If the rift had truly fractured space-time, then the Challenger might exist in multiple realities at once. The visions people were experiencing weren't just alternate histories—they were windows into other versions of reality where the disaster had never occurred.

As the days passed, more survivors of the Challenger program began to experience these strange phenomena. Some reported brief moments where they seemed to slip into an alternate timeline entirely, only to snap back to their current reality seconds later. Others described seeing people who had died in the explosion, alive and well, as if they had never been lost.

June Scobee Rodgers had one particularly vivid experience while walking through a park. For a moment, she swore she saw Francis standing by a tree, waving to her, as though he had just returned from space. The moment was fleeting, but it felt so real that she couldn't shake the feeling that, somewhere, in some version of the universe, he was still alive.

Roger Boisjoly, too, was plagued by the same feeling. He began to experience long stretches of time where he could no longer distinguish between the real timeline and the alternate reality he was seeing. In these moments, he saw himself giving a successful presentation about the Challenger's flawless mission, a future where his warnings about the O-rings had been heeded, and the shuttle had never exploded.

The rift had torn more than just a hole in space-time—it had fractured reality itself. And now, those who had been closest to the disaster were beginning to feel its effects.

As Hayes and his team continued their investigation, they realized that the rift's influence was growing. The visions were becoming more frequent, more powerful, and they were starting to affect more people. The boundaries between timelines were weakening, and soon, it wouldn't just be survivors of the Challenger program who were affected.

The world was beginning to experience fragments of the future—pieces of alternate realities bleeding through into their own. And as these fragments grew stronger, the team knew they were running out of time.

The rift was still open. And if they didn't find a way to close it, reality itself might unravel.

Chapter 22: The Secret Files

The world remained fixated on the Challenger disaster, with the official narrative slowly taking shape through public hearings and reports. The Rogers Commission had all but concluded that human error and mechanical failure were to blame. For most, the tragedy was a sobering reminder of the risks involved in space exploration. But beneath the surface, cracks in the official story were beginning to show.

Rumors had already been circulating among insiders—whispers of classified information and strange anomalies that NASA had been desperate to keep under wraps. These whispers grew louder when, in a shocking turn of events, a NASA whistleblower emerged, leaking a series of classified documents that would send shockwaves through the agency and the intelligence community.

It started with an anonymous email sent to several journalists and a select few within NASA. The email included a cryptic message: **"The Challenger disaster wasn't an accident. The truth is buried in the files. Ask the right questions."** Attached were several heavily redacted documents, their origins marked as "TOP SECRET: EYES ONLY." The information within these files hinted at something much darker—a government group that had anticipated the explosion long before the Challenger launched.

The leaked documents quickly found their way to Dr. Allan Hayes and his team, who had been quietly investigating the anomalies surrounding the disaster. The files were incomplete and fragmented, but even in their heavily redacted state, they painted a picture of a covert group operating at the highest levels of government—a group that had been monitoring the Challenger mission for reasons that went far beyond mechanical failure.

Hayes sat in his office late at night, staring at the documents. Eliza Langston and Mark Whittaker were with him, equally stunned by what they had just read.

"This can't be real," Eliza said, flipping through one of the files. "If these documents are legitimate, it means the government knew something like this was going to happen."

"Not just knew," Hayes replied, his voice tight with disbelief. "They were planning for it."

Whittaker leaned back in his chair, his face hardening as he studied the papers. "It explains a lot, actually. The way we've been stonewalled, the missing telemetry data, the classified reports that never made it into the official investigation. They were covering something up from the beginning."

The documents, though cryptic, mentioned a secretive group known only as *The Committee*. It appeared to be a loose network of military and intelligence officials, scientists, and government contractors who operated under direct orders from a shadowy branch of the U.S. government. The Committee's existence had never been made public, and even within NASA, only a handful of people knew of its operations. According to the files, The Committee had been involved in high-risk space missions for years, monitoring them not just for mechanical failures but for potential encounters with unknown phenomena.

The most alarming revelation was that The Committee had been closely watching the Challenger mission. One document, marked **Eyes Only: Special Operations**, referenced unexplained anomalies detected by government satellites days before the launch. The document suggested that certain high-level officials had anticipated that the mission could encounter an event of unprecedented significance—something that might alter the very fabric of space-time.

One file in particular stood out to Hayes. It was a heavily redacted memo that seemed to summarize a briefing given to The Committee just a few weeks before the Challenger launch. Though much of the content was blacked out, a few sentences remained intact:

"The presence of anomalous signals in low Earth orbit cannot be ignored. These signals match previous patterns observed during classified operations. There is a strong possibility that STS-51L [the Challenger mission] will encounter similar phenomena. Preparations for containment are in place should an event occur."

Hayes felt a cold chill settle over him as he read the words. This group—the shadowy figures behind The Committee—had known. They had known the Challenger was heading into dangerous, unknown territory, and yet they had let the mission proceed. Worse still, they had prepared for it.

"They expected something to happen," Hayes said quietly, his hands gripping the memo. "They knew about the anomalies, and they let the launch go ahead anyway."

Eliza's face went pale. "They let the crew die. They sacrificed them."

The implications were staggering. The Challenger disaster wasn't just a tragic accident caused by faulty O-rings and cold weather—it had been foreseen. And the government, or at least a select few within it, had done nothing to stop it. In fact, it appeared they had been waiting for it.

Whittaker sifted through another document, this one a technical report detailing the analysis of the energy spikes that had been detected before the explosion. Though much of the report was redacted, the remaining text suggested that these spikes had been recorded during other missions—classified missions that had encountered similar anomalies. The report hinted at a deeper investigation into what these energy signatures represented, though any concrete conclusions were blacked out.

"What's their endgame?" Whittaker asked, his voice tense. "Why monitor these anomalies and not do anything to stop the launch? What could they possibly gain from letting the shuttle explode?"

Hayes didn't have an answer. The Committee's motives remained unclear, but the documents made one thing certain: they had been watching for something. The energy spikes, the gravitational distortions, and the strange telemetry glitches were part of a pattern—one that The Committee had been tracking for years.

"They weren't just watching for an explosion," Hayes said slowly. "They were watching for a specific event. The rift."

Eliza's eyes widened. "The dimensional rift?"

"Think about it," Hayes continued. "The Challenger didn't just explode—it encountered something. The energy readings we've been tracking, the satellite data, even the strange visions people are having... they all point to one thing. The shuttle crossed into another dimension. And The Committee knew it was possible. They wanted to see what would happen."

The weight of his words hung in the air. The Challenger had become more than just a space mission—it had become a test, a way for this elite group to observe the effects of a dimensional rift. And the crew had been the unwitting subjects of this experiment.

Whittaker closed the document he was holding and stood up, pacing the room. "So now what? We have these files, but there's no way we can go public with this. If The Committee is real, they'll bury us before we even have a chance to blow the whistle."

"We need more proof," Hayes said, his mind racing. "There's got to be something else—more files, more data. We need to find out who leaked these documents and if there's more where this came from."

Eliza nodded. "If we can find the source, we might be able to get the full picture. But we have to be careful. If The Committee really is pulling the strings, they won't let us keep digging for long."

As the team prepared to follow the new lead, they knew they were walking a dangerous line. The Committee had the power to shape the narrative, to hide the truth from the world. And now that Hayes and his team had stumbled upon their secrets, they were no longer just investigators—they were targets.

The whistleblower had given them a glimpse into a shadowy world, but it was up to them to uncover the full truth. They would have to move quickly and quietly, navigating a labyrinth of classified files and hidden agendas.

The Challenger disaster had been a tragedy—but it had also been a catalyst. The rift was still open, and now, with The Committee watching their every move, Hayes and his team were about to uncover the deepest, darkest secrets that NASA—and the world—had ever known.

And the truth would change everything.

Chapter 23: The Phantom Crew

In the weeks following the Challenger disaster, the families of the fallen astronauts had been overwhelmed with grief, struggling to find solace in a tragedy that seemed too immense to fully comprehend. Public tributes, memorial services, and constant media coverage had left them emotionally drained, but there had been no true closure. The remains of the crew were never fully recovered, and while NASA had offered its official explanations, something felt unfinished, unsettled, as if part of the story was still waiting to be told.

It was during this period of mourning that the families began receiving mysterious, unsettling visits.

June Scobee Rodgers, the widow of Commander Francis Scobee, was one of the first to be approached. It happened late one evening, after the media attention had finally quieted down. She had been trying to rebuild a sense of normalcy in her life, but nothing was the same without Francis. Her nights were filled with sleepless hours and memories of her husband. Then, one night, the knock on her door came.

The man who stood on her doorstep wore a plain black suit, his expression cold and unreadable. He wasn't someone June recognized, but he didn't seem like a typical visitor. He held no flowers, no condolences—only a small envelope.

"Mrs. Scobee," he said in a low, even tone, "I represent a group with information that may be of interest to you."

June's heart raced. She instinctively stepped back, wary of the stranger, but something about his demeanor made her pause. He extended the envelope toward her.

"Your husband's mission didn't end the way you've been told," the man continued. "We believe there's a possibility that the crew of the Challenger... may still be alive."

Her breath caught in her throat. She was certain she had misheard him. "What are you talking about? The explosion—there's no way anyone could have survived."

The man didn't flinch. "Not in this reality. But we've uncovered evidence that suggests they were transported elsewhere. To another dimension. And there's a chance they may still be alive—trapped, but alive."

June stared at the envelope, her hands trembling. Every instinct told her to shut the door, to push this man and his wild theories away. But her heart ached with the faint, impossible hope that he might be telling the truth.

"Who are you?" she finally asked, her voice shaking.

"We're part of a group investigating certain... phenomena," the man said, his words carefully chosen. "We don't operate within official channels, and we're not part of NASA. But we've been tracking the anomalies surrounding the Challenger disaster, and we believe the crew encountered something far more significant than a mechanical failure."

June's mind raced. She had heard the rumors—whispers of strange energy spikes, of unexplained events before and after the explosion. But she had dismissed them as conspiracy theories, the desperate speculation of those who couldn't accept the tragedy.

Now, this stranger was standing in front of her, suggesting something far more unimaginable. The crew hadn't died—they had been transported to another dimension.

"I don't believe you," June said, her voice faltering.

The man's expression didn't change. "I understand your skepticism. But inside that envelope is a document that outlines our findings. We've been tracking the anomalies for years, long before the Challenger launch. And recently, we've picked up signals—signals that suggest the crew may be trying to communicate."

He placed the envelope in her hand and turned to leave, but paused before stepping away. "You're not the only one we've contacted. The other families are being informed as well. There's more to this story, Mrs. Scobee. Don't close the door on it just yet."

Without another word, he disappeared into the night, leaving June standing in the doorway, the envelope clutched tightly in her hand. For a long time, she didn't move. She couldn't. Her mind was spinning with disbelief, hope, and fear.

The envelope remained unopened on her kitchen table for hours, as June wrestled with whether to open it or throw it away. But in the end, she couldn't resist. She carefully tore it open and pulled out a single sheet of paper. The document was sparse, filled with technical jargon she didn't fully understand, but one phrase stood out, highlighted in red: **"Dimensional Displacement – Potential for Recovery."**

June's hands shook as she read the final lines: **"Further investigation into the possibility of the crew's survival is ongoing. Initial findings suggest contact may be possible."**

Elsewhere, similar encounters were taking place.

Roger McNair, brother of Mission Specialist Ronald McNair, had been visited by a different figure—this one a woman in a grey coat who approached him in a coffee shop. She had spoken in hushed tones, offering him the same message: **"Your brother may still be alive, but in another dimension."**

The family of Christa McAuliffe, the schoolteacher who had inspired millions with her selection for the mission, received an encrypted message delivered to their home. The message contained detailed coordinates and a brief note: **"Search for the signal."**

The families were being drawn into a web of secrets and half-truths, their grief compounded by a growing sense of unease. Some dismissed the mysterious visitors as cruel hoaxes, preying on their sorrow. But others couldn't shake the feeling that there was something more to these claims.

As word spread among the families, a quiet desperation took hold. Meetings were arranged in secret, whispers exchanged about the strange visitors and the cryptic messages. Some of the families shared the documents they had received, comparing notes, searching for any shred of truth.

June Scobee found herself drawn into these clandestine meetings, her skepticism wavering as more families reported similar encounters. The stories were eerily consistent—shadowy figures offering hope that the crew was still alive, trapped in a place beyond their understanding.

But none of it made sense. How could the crew be alive when they had witnessed the explosion? How could they be in another dimension?

As the families dug deeper, they began to realize that these shadowy figures were connected to the same secretive group that Hayes and his team had been investigating—*The Committee*. This group had known about the anomalies long before the Challenger launch, and now it seemed they were reaching out to the families, suggesting that the crew's fate was far from sealed.

June couldn't let go of the possibility, as slim as it seemed. Could Francis still be alive, out there somewhere, waiting to come home? She needed answers.

And so, she decided to confront the only people who might know the truth. She contacted Hayes and his team, who had been following the trail of The Committee and the dimensional rift.

When Hayes met with June in a quiet, secluded café, she told him everything—the mysterious visitor, the document, and the claim that Francis might still be alive. Hayes listened carefully, and when she finished, he nodded gravely.

"You're not the first to tell me this," he said, his voice filled with concern. "We've been tracking these rumors, and we've uncovered evidence that points to the existence of a rift—a tear in the fabric of space-time. If what we've found is true, then it's possible the crew wasn't destroyed in the explosion. They were displaced. Sent somewhere else."

June's heart pounded in her chest. "Can they come back?"

"We don't know," Hayes admitted. "But we're trying to find out."

As Hayes and his team continued their investigation, they realized that The Committee wasn't just hiding the truth—they were actively searching for a way to recover the crew from the rift. The signals they had detected were growing stronger, and the possibility of contact was becoming more real.

The families of the Challenger crew were left with a painful, impossible hope: that their loved ones might still be out there, somewhere, waiting to return from the phantom world in which they had been trapped.

But as they pressed for answers, they knew they were entering dangerous territory. The truth about the Challenger disaster was far more complex than they had ever imagined, and now, they were caught in the center of a conspiracy that spanned dimensions.

The Challenger crew might still be alive. But if they were, their rescue would be the most dangerous mission humanity had ever attempted.

Chapter 24: The Ghost Shuttle

In the dimly lit NASA control room, a small group of engineers and scientists stared at the data on their screens, their expressions filled with confusion and disbelief. For the past several days, they had been receiving strange, intermittent signals—weak, distorted, and unlike anything they had encountered before. The source of the signals was even more baffling. Based on their trajectory and timing, it appeared that these signals were coming from the *Challenger* itself.

But that was impossible.

The *Challenger* had been destroyed months earlier, and the crew had perished in the explosion. Yet, here they were, staring at telemetry that suggested something else—something that defied logic.

The signals weren't continuous, nor were they clear. They came in bursts, fragments of data transmitted in erratic intervals. At first, they were dismissed as random noise or interference from other satellites. But as the patterns became more distinct, NASA technicians began to suspect that they were dealing with something far stranger.

One of the engineers, a young woman named Dana Walker, was the first to recognize the possibility. Late one night, after hours of analyzing the strange signals, she noticed a distinct signature buried within the noise. It was faint, but unmistakable—the *Challenger*'s original communications frequency. At first, she couldn't believe it. The shuttle's systems had been obliterated in the explosion, its components scattered across the Atlantic. But here, in the middle of this strange signal, was evidence that the shuttle—or something that had once been the shuttle—was still transmitting.

"Look at this," Dana whispered to her colleague, Matthew Flores, who had been monitoring nearby satellite activity. "This can't be right. This frequency... it's from the *Challenger*."

Matthew frowned, leaning closer to the screen. "That's not possible. The *Challenger* is gone. There's no way it could be transmitting anything."

"I know," Dana replied, her voice tight with uncertainty. "But the signal is real. And it's not random. Look at the data stream—it's fragmented, but it's there."

Matthew stared at the screen in disbelief. The signal was faint, distorted, but beneath the static, he could see the unmistakable signs of telemetry. Coordinates. System readouts. But they didn't make sense—some of the data was decades old, as if it had been stuck in a time loop, while other fragments seemed to be from an entirely different mission.

"What the hell is this?" he muttered, running a hand through his hair.

Dana's mind raced. There was only one explanation that made sense, even though it defied everything they knew about physics and space travel. The *Challenger* hadn't simply exploded—it had been displaced, torn between dimensions or caught in some kind of temporal anomaly. And now, somehow, it was trying to communicate from wherever it had been trapped.

They needed more data. Dana quickly isolated the signal and began running diagnostics to determine its source and strength. The results were inconclusive—the signal was bouncing off multiple satellites, making it nearly impossible to pinpoint its origin. But one thing was clear: it wasn't coming from Earth.

Later that evening, Dana and Matthew brought the discovery to their supervisor, Dr. Allan Hayes, who had been quietly investigating the Challenger anomaly for months. When they showed him the signal, his face darkened with recognition.

"We've been picking up similar signals for a while now," Hayes admitted, his voice grim. "They're weak and fragmented, but there's a pattern. It's as if the shuttle is still out there, caught in some kind of... temporal distortion."

"Temporal distortion?" Matthew repeated, incredulous. "You're saying the *Challenger* is stuck in time?"

"Not exactly," Hayes replied, pulling up additional data on his own console. "What we're seeing is evidence that the shuttle didn't just explode. It was displaced—torn out of our reality and into another. The signals you're picking up could be coming from that other dimension, or from some version of the *Challenger* that exists in a fractured timeline."

Dana's heart raced. It was the same theory that had been haunting them since the strange visitors began approaching the crew's families. Could it be true? Could the *Challenger* and its crew still be out there, somewhere between realities, trying to make contact?

"We need to run a deep analysis on this," Hayes continued, pulling up data from a nearby satellite monitoring system. "These signals are faint, but they're growing more frequent. If the shuttle is trying to communicate, we need to figure out how to respond."

For the next several hours, the team worked in near silence, combing through the distorted transmissions and trying to piece together a coherent message. It was slow, painstaking work—most of the signal was garbled beyond recognition, and whatever data they could extract seemed out of sync with normal time.

But then, Dana noticed something that sent chills down her spine. One of the signal fragments contained a brief voice transmission. It was barely audible, hidden beneath layers of static, but as she isolated the audio and enhanced it, a voice emerged.

It was faint, distorted by time and distance, but unmistakable.

"This is Commander Francis Scobee of the *Challenger*... requesting assistance... we're... unable to..."

The message cut off abruptly, leaving nothing but static in its wake. Dana's heart pounded as the reality of what she had just heard sank in.

It was Francis Scobee's voice—the voice of a man who had died months ago, speaking as if he were still aboard the shuttle, still alive, still waiting for help.

"Did you hear that?" she whispered, her voice trembling.

Hayes leaned in, his face pale with shock. "It's him," he whispered. "He's alive."

Matthew shook his head in disbelief. "No, that's impossible. This has to be a recording—some kind of distortion in the signal."

"It's not a recording," Dana said firmly. "The timestamp on the transmission doesn't match anything from the original mission logs. It's as if he's speaking now, from wherever the shuttle is."

Hayes nodded slowly. "The *Challenger* isn't just lost. It's stuck in some kind of temporal rift, looping between realities. And the crew—they're still trying to reach us."

The realization hit the team like a cold wave. The *Challenger*, the shuttle that the world believed had been destroyed in a fiery explosion, was still out there—trapped in a fractured reality, its crew alive but isolated, their voices reaching out across the void.

But there was something else, something even more unsettling. The transmissions weren't consistent. The voices they were hearing were sometimes distorted by time, as if they were fragments of a future that had never come to pass. In some of the signal bursts, Scobee's voice sounded clear, as if he were still in command of the shuttle, carrying out a successful mission. In others, his voice was faint, filled with desperation, as if he were trapped in a world where the shuttle had never escaped its doomed fate.

The *Challenger* was caught in a time loop, its crew lost between dimensions, unable to move forward or return home. And now, NASA had a choice to make.

"We have to find a way to respond," Dana said, her voice urgent. "If the crew is still out there, we can't just leave them."

Hayes nodded. "We will. But we need to be careful. Whatever caused the rift could still be active. We're dealing with forces we barely understand."

As the team prepared to decode more of the transmissions, they knew they were on the verge of uncovering something far greater than anyone had imagined. The *Challenger* had become more than just a shuttle—it was a ghost ship, sailing between worlds, carrying its crew through fractured time.

But the question remained: could they bring the *Challenger* home, or would it remain lost in the void forever?

As they continued their investigation, they realized that the signals were growing stronger. The *Challenger* was reaching out, calling to them across the dimensions. And now, they had to find a way to answer.

The ghost shuttle was waiting.

Chapter 25: A Rift Expands

Cape Canaveral had always been a symbol of human ambition and the endless pursuit of exploration, but now, something far darker and more unexplainable was unfolding along its shores. In the months following the Challenger disaster and the emergence of strange signals from the shuttle, the area around the spaceport had become a hotspot for increasingly bizarre and terrifying phenomena.

The rift, once contained to the disaster itself, was expanding.

It started small—local residents near the launch site reported seeing strange lights in the sky, eerie flickers that seemed to vanish as quickly as they appeared. Some described seeing brief flashes of the Challenger itself, as if the shuttle had reappeared for a split second before fading back into whatever void it had been pulled into. These sightings were dismissed at first as the aftereffects of trauma or imagination running wild, but as the weeks went on, the occurrences became harder to ignore.

One night, a security guard stationed near the Kennedy Space Center reported something more troubling. As he patrolled the perimeter near Launch Complex 39, where the Challenger had once stood, he saw what appeared to be a full-scale shuttle sitting on the pad, bathed in moonlight. At first, he assumed it was part of a new launch preparation, but as he got closer, the shuttle flickered—like an image on a malfunctioning television screen—before vanishing entirely. He swore he could still hear the hum of engines and the faint, crackling echoes of voices over the radio.

Word spread quickly. The phenomenon wasn't limited to just the Challenger. People began to report seeing vehicles and objects that didn't belong, strange weather events that lasted only moments, and even figures—humans—that appeared briefly, as though they had wandered in from some alternate version of reality.

NASA, already struggling with the weight of the official Challenger investigation, quietly set up a task force to monitor these phenomena. The classified group included Dr. Allan Hayes, Dana Walker, and Matthew Flores—each of them now deeply invested in understanding the expanding rift and what it could mean for the future. Alongside them was Eliza Langston, whose knowledge of the scientific anomalies surrounding the rift made her indispensable to the investigation.

They were working against time, and against something they were only beginning to understand.

Sitting in a makeshift operations center on the outskirts of Cape Canaveral, the team gathered around a bank of monitors displaying satellite imagery, radar readings, and live reports coming in from locals and security personnel. The data was overwhelming. Unexplained power surges, disruptions in communications, and electromagnetic spikes were becoming frequent occurrences. But the most alarming discovery was that the phenomena were spreading beyond Cape Canaveral—reaching further and further inland.

"The rift is expanding," Eliza said, her voice filled with tension. "Whatever it was that happened to the Challenger, it's affecting more than just the shuttle. It's pulling in everything around it—objects, people, even time itself. The boundaries between realities are starting to blur."

Hayes frowned, staring at the readings on the monitor. "We've been picking up strange electromagnetic signatures, consistent with the energy spikes that occurred during the launch. But they're not just coming from one location anymore—they're spreading. And fast."

Dana, who had been monitoring the strange transmissions still being picked up from the Challenger, leaned in closer to the conversation. "Are we saying that the rift could affect the entire region? Could it keep spreading?"

Eliza nodded gravely. "If it's not contained, yes. Right now, it's localized to Cape Canaveral, but the patterns are expanding. It's as if the tear in space-time is growing wider, drawing in everything around it. The longer it remains open, the more unstable it becomes."

Matthew, who had been tracking the reports of sightings around the area, spoke up. "I've been collecting reports from locals. People are seeing things—vehicles, aircraft, and even buildings that shouldn't exist. We've even had a few reports of people claiming they've seen versions of themselves. Duplicates."

Hayes looked up, alarmed. "Duplicates? You mean people are encountering versions of themselves from other timelines?"

Matthew nodded, his expression grim. "It sounds crazy, but the reports are consistent. They describe seeing brief flashes of themselves, almost like a reflection in a mirror, except it's not just a reflection. It's... them. Standing there, in the flesh, for just a moment, before disappearing."

The implications were terrifying. The rift wasn't just affecting objects and technology—it was distorting the very fabric of human existence, pulling in alternate versions of people, places, and events from different realities.

"What about the people who've gone missing?" Dana asked, glancing at her notes. "We've had at least three reports of individuals disappearing near the launch site, only to reappear a few hours later, completely disoriented. They claimed they were somewhere else, in a version of Cape Canaveral that looked different—older, but still familiar. One of them swore they saw the Challenger getting ready for launch."

Eliza rubbed her temples, her mind racing. "It's possible that those who disappear are slipping into alternate dimensions, caught between different realities. The rift is breaking down the barriers between timelines, allowing brief crossings between them."

Hayes stood up, pacing the room. "We need to contain this. If the rift keeps expanding, we're looking at a catastrophe on a scale we can't predict. It's not just about bringing the Challenger crew back anymore. If we don't stop this, entire timelines could collapse into each other."

But how could they stop something that they barely understood? The rift was a force beyond anything they had encountered, a tear in the fabric of reality that defied the laws of physics. And now it was spreading, growing stronger with every passing day.

As the team worked frantically to analyze the data, more reports poured in. Civilians were seeing strange apparitions along the coastline—ships from long-forgotten eras, cars that flickered in and out of existence, even buildings that had been demolished years ago suddenly reappearing, only to vanish minutes later. There were whispers of entire streets temporarily being overrun with ghostly figures—people in clothes from different time periods, walking aimlessly before fading away.

Then came the most terrifying report yet.

Late one night, a team of NASA security officers patrolling near the launch complex spotted something hovering just above the water's edge. At first, it looked like a cloud of mist or fog, but as they got closer, they saw it was something else entirely—a distorted, shimmering mass that seemed to pulse with energy. As they approached, they realized it was an object. A shuttle.

The *Challenger*.

It was incomplete—flickering in and out of existence, as though it were trapped between two realities, frozen in the moment of its destruction and restoration. They could hear faint voices, distorted radio chatter, but the image dissolved before they could get any closer.

When the report reached Hayes and his team, they knew they were running out of time.

"We're dealing with a collapse," Eliza said, her voice steady but filled with dread. "The rift is widening, and it's pulling entire fragments of alternate timelines into our reality. If we don't find a way to close it soon, the entire region—maybe even the entire world—could become a patchwork of broken realities."

Hayes nodded grimly. "We need to find the source of the rift and figure out a way to reverse it. Whatever it takes."

But the question loomed large: How could they stop something that had already begun to unravel time and space itself?

The rift was expanding, and with every day that passed, the line between realities grew thinner, more fragile. The sightings of objects and events from alternate worlds were no longer confined to Cape Canaveral—they were beginning to appear in nearby towns, and it was only a matter of time before they spread further.

The team had one last chance to stop the rift before it consumed everything. But to do that, they would need to understand the full scope of the phenomenon—and face the possibility that the Challenger crew, still lost in the void, might hold the key to saving their world.

Chapter 26: The Convergence Theory

The situation at Cape Canaveral had become increasingly dire. Strange phenomena continued to intensify, with sightings of objects and people from alternate realities becoming more frequent. Buildings and landscapes shifted, only to return to normal moments later. In some cases, entire sections of the coastline flickered between different versions of themselves—sometimes appearing as they had been in the 1960s, other times as futuristic visions that defied explanation. It was clear that the rift, once believed to be localized, was now spreading beyond control.

Desperate for answers, NASA reached out to some of the world's leading physicists—experts in theoretical physics, quantum mechanics, and the nature of space-time. These scientists had been aware of the Challenger's anomalies for some time, following the strange reports but never fully understanding what they were dealing with. Now, as the phenomena grew more intense, they gathered at NASA's headquarters to present a new, terrifying theory: **The Convergence Theory**.

Dr. Adrian Keller, a brilliant physicist known for his work in quantum theory, was among the first to speak. He stood in front of a group of NASA officials, Hayes, Eliza Langston, and the task force that had been investigating the rift, his expression grave. Keller had long been skeptical of wild theories about dimensional rifts and parallel worlds, but now, the evidence was undeniable.

"We've been analyzing the data from the strange phenomena near Cape Canaveral," Keller began, gesturing to the holographic display behind him, which showed satellite imagery, energy readings, and simulations of the rift's expansion. "At first, we believed this was an isolated anomaly—a tear in the fabric of space-time caused by the Challenger explosion. But what we're seeing now suggests something much larger."

He clicked a button, and the screen shifted to a complex model of space-time, represented as a web of interconnected dimensions.

"The Challenger's explosion didn't just tear through space-time," Keller continued. "It triggered a **convergence**—a moment where two parallel realities, which normally exist side by side, began to bleed into each other. The explosion acted as a catalyst, weakening the barriers between these dimensions and causing them to overlap."

The room was silent as Keller's words sank in. Hayes, who had been following this theory for months, felt the weight of it finally come crashing down.

"What you're saying," Hayes said slowly, "is that the rift isn't just a tear. It's causing two realities—two timelines—to merge."

Keller nodded grimly. "Exactly. We've long theorized that alternate realities exist—parallel universes where different versions of events play out. Normally, these dimensions remain separate, with no way to interact. But the explosion, combined with the energy spikes we've been tracking, created a weak point in space-time. And now, these two realities are converging."

He paused, letting the gravity of the situation sink in. "This convergence is what's causing the strange phenomena around Cape Canaveral. People are seeing objects and events from alternate realities because those timelines are bleeding into our own. In some cases, they're even seeing themselves—alternate versions, drawn from a different reality where their lives played out differently."

The screen behind Keller shifted again, displaying a map of the anomalies around Cape Canaveral. The red zones where the phenomena were most intense formed a clear pattern, spiraling outward from the site of the Challenger's explosion.

"This is the epicenter of the rift," Keller said, pointing to the map. "It's where the convergence is strongest. But the disturbing part is that the rift is expanding. As the two realities bleed into each other, the boundary between them grows weaker. If we don't stop this, it's possible that the two realities could fully merge."

Dana Walker, who had been monitoring the signals from the Challenger, leaned forward, her brow furrowed. "What happens if they merge completely?"

Keller's expression darkened. "If the convergence reaches critical mass, the two realities will no longer be distinct. They will overlap entirely. People, objects, and events from both realities will coexist in the same space, but with no clear division between them. It could lead to widespread chaos—confusion, structural collapse, even the possibility of paradoxes."

The room was silent as everyone absorbed the implications. If the two realities fully converged, the world could be plunged into a state of complete disarray, where the past, present, and future from two dimensions existed simultaneously. It would be impossible to predict what would happen next.

"Has this ever happened before?" Matthew Flores asked, his voice filled with tension.

Keller shook his head. "Not on this scale. We've seen small instances of quantum entanglement, where particles from different dimensions interact, but nothing like this. If the convergence continues unchecked, it could become a permanent rupture—a gateway between worlds. And once that happens, we may not be able to close it."

Eliza, who had been studying the anomalies for months, spoke up. "But why now? What was it about the Challenger explosion that caused this? We've had space shuttle disasters before, but nothing like this has ever happened."

Keller hesitated before answering. "We don't fully understand the mechanisms at play, but we believe the explosion occurred at a critical point in space-time—a weak spot, if you will. The energy released during the explosion, combined with the gravitational forces at play, was enough to tear through the fabric of reality. It's possible that this weak point was always there, just waiting for the right conditions to open the rift."

"But what about the crew?" Dana asked, her voice trembling slightly. "We've been receiving signals from the Challenger. Could they still be alive, trapped in the other dimension?"

Keller nodded. "It's possible. The convergence could have displaced the shuttle and its crew into the parallel reality. If that's the case, they may be experiencing their own version of events—an alternate timeline where the disaster never happened. But in our reality, they're lost between worlds, trying to communicate through the rift."

Hayes exhaled sharply. The idea that the Challenger crew might still be alive, trapped in a different dimension, was both thrilling and terrifying. They had been chasing those signals for weeks, hoping for answers, but now it seemed that their worst fears were being confirmed.

"If they're still out there," Hayes said, "we have to find a way to bring them back."

Keller nodded. "We're working on a plan to stabilize the rift, but it's risky. If we disrupt the convergence too soon, we could collapse both realities, causing a complete breakdown. We need more time to analyze the data and come up with a solution."

"Time is the one thing we don't have," Eliza muttered. "The convergence is spreading faster every day. We've already had reports of anomalies as far inland as Orlando. If we wait too long, we might lose control completely."

Keller's face tightened. "We're doing everything we can, but this is uncharted territory. The convergence is unpredictable, and we don't know what will happen if we try to interfere. The risks are enormous."

Hayes glanced at the map of anomalies, his mind racing. "We need to try something. If we don't, the convergence will swallow everything."

The meeting ended with no clear solution in sight, but the team knew they were on borrowed time. The convergence wasn't just a theory anymore—it was a reality, one that was quickly spiraling out of control. Two dimensions were bleeding into each other, and unless they found a way to stop it, the rift would continue to grow, merging their world with another.

As they worked through the night, monitoring the expanding rift and preparing for the next phase of their mission, Hayes, Dana, Eliza, and the rest of the team knew that the Challenger's fate wasn't just a mystery to be solved—it was the key to saving their world from complete collapse.

But with the convergence growing stronger, they had to face the possibility that they were already too late.

Chapter 27: Temporal Instability

The eerie phenomena surrounding Cape Canaveral had taken on a new, more terrifying dimension: time itself had begun to unravel.

For weeks, the strange reports of alternate realities, ghostly apparitions, and inexplicable anomalies had gripped the region, but now, something even more disturbing was happening. People living near the Challenger launch site started experiencing time in ways that defied all logic. The rift that had been expanding since the disaster was no longer just affecting space—it was bending time, warping it into something unrecognizable.

The first reports were subtle. Residents near the Kennedy Space Center would lose track of minutes or even hours, waking from what seemed like a brief nap to find entire days had passed. In other cases, people would suddenly remember events that hadn't happened—at least, not in this reality. Memories overlapped in confusing ways, blending together moments from their own lives with events that seemed to belong to someone else.

June Scobee Rodgers, still grappling with the possibility that her husband, Commander Francis Scobee, might be alive in another dimension, was one of the first to experience the growing temporal instability. One afternoon, as she walked through her home, she suddenly found herself standing in a different room. At first, she assumed she had just been lost in thought, but the unsettling feeling lingered. The clock on her wall showed that three hours had passed—hours she couldn't account for.

The next day, she experienced something even stranger. As she was preparing dinner, a sudden wave of dizziness hit her. When she blinked, she was no longer in her kitchen but outside, standing near the tree where she had last spoken to Francis before his mission. The memory was vivid, but something was wrong—she could hear Francis's voice, faint but real, as if he were standing right there, speaking to her from across time.

And then, just as quickly, she was back in her kitchen, her hands trembling. She looked at the clock again. Another hour had passed, yet it felt like only a moment.

She wasn't alone.

Across Cape Canaveral, others began reporting similar experiences. A local fisherman claimed he had gone out on his boat one morning, only to return home at sunset, unable to remember anything that had happened in between. A group of tourists visiting the Space Center reported seeing the Challenger on the launchpad, preparing for its ill-fated mission—except it had already exploded decades ago. Even security personnel, trained to remain calm in extreme situations, began filing reports of time shifts and "phantom" memories that seemed to bleed through from another reality.

At NASA, the situation had reached a breaking point. The task force led by Dr. Allan Hayes and his team was working day and night, but every time they thought they were getting closer to understanding the rift, new anomalies emerged. The convergence of two realities had triggered something far worse than anyone had anticipated—time itself was beginning to break down, and it was spreading beyond the launch site.

Dana Walker, who had been monitoring the signals from the *Challenger*, was growing increasingly worried. The transmissions from the shuttle, once faint and sporadic, were becoming more frequent and more distorted. Some of the signals seemed to loop, repeating fragments of communication from the doomed mission, while others carried messages that hadn't been recorded during the launch—messages that seemed to come from a future that hadn't yet occurred.

"This is getting out of control," Dana said, her voice tense as she watched the latest telemetry. "We're seeing overlapping timelines, signals coming from both past and future events. The rift is creating a temporal echo, and it's spreading faster than we can track."

Dr. Eliza Langston, who had been studying the nature of the rift, leaned over the data. "It's worse than we thought. The temporal instability isn't just isolated to Cape Canaveral anymore. We've had reports from nearby towns—people are losing hours, even days. And some are experiencing events from entirely different points in time."

Matthew Flores, who had been collecting reports of the temporal anomalies, added, "We've got multiple cases of people claiming they've seen themselves—like they're meeting their past or future selves in real time. And they're not just seeing them—they're interacting with them, only to have those interactions vanish minutes later. It's as if time is folding in on itself."

The team knew they were dealing with a disaster of unprecedented proportions. Time, once a fixed and unyielding force, was now fluid, behaving unpredictably. The boundaries between past, present, and future were collapsing, and the rift was expanding its reach.

"The convergence is accelerating," Hayes said, pacing the room as he reviewed the latest reports. "We're seeing overlapping realities, but now, time itself is collapsing. If we don't stabilize the rift soon, we could be looking at a complete breakdown of time in this area—maybe even beyond."

Eliza shook her head. "But how do we stabilize something like this? We've never dealt with anything like it. It's not just space that's distorted; it's time. Every second that passes, the instability grows."

The team was running out of options. With the rift spreading and the temporal anomalies becoming more severe, they knew that simply monitoring the situation wasn't enough. They needed to act, but they didn't know how.

Then, something unexpected happened.

While scanning the latest data, Dana picked up a new signal—stronger and clearer than anything they had detected before.

At first, she thought it was another loop, but as she adjusted the frequency, she realized this was different. It was a live transmission.

"It's the *Challenger*," Dana said, her voice barely above a whisper. "They're transmitting again."

The room fell silent as they listened. The voice on the other end was unmistakable: Commander Francis Scobee.

"This is Commander Scobee of the *Challenger*. We're experiencing severe... temporal instability. We... can't find our way back. Do you copy? Can anyone hear us?"

Hayes felt a cold chill run down his spine. It was Scobee, speaking as if the explosion had never happened, as if the shuttle and its crew were still alive, trapped in the temporal rift.

"We're receiving you, Commander," Hayes said into the radio, his voice calm despite the chaos around them. "What's your status? Can you give us any information about your location?"

There was a long pause, filled with static and distortion. Then, Scobee's voice came through again, more fragmented this time.

"We... think we're caught in some kind of... temporal loop. Every time we try to... correct our course, we end up back where we started. It's like... time isn't moving forward. We're stuck. I don't know how much longer... we can hold on."

The transmission cut off, leaving only static behind.

The team exchanged uneasy glances. The *Challenger* and its crew were alive, but they were trapped in a temporal limbo, caught between realities and unable to escape. The rift had displaced them not just in space, but in time, and now, the same instability was spreading across Cape Canaveral.

"We need to find a way to pull them out," Hayes said, his voice firm. "They're stuck in the rift, but if we can stabilize the temporal distortion, we might be able to bring them back."

"But how do we do that?" Dana asked. "We don't even fully understand how the rift works."

Eliza spoke up, her voice filled with determination. "We need to disrupt the convergence. If we can reverse the flow of energy at the epicenter of the rift—the site of the Challenger explosion—we might be able to stop the temporal instability from spreading. It's risky, but it's our best shot."

The team quickly got to work, devising a plan to stabilize the rift and reverse the temporal flow. It was a race against time—quite literally. With the convergence accelerating and temporal anomalies becoming more widespread, they knew they didn't have long before the instability reached a point of no return.

As they prepared for the operation, Hayes couldn't help but feel a deep sense of urgency. The crew of the *Challenger* was still out there, lost in time, waiting for rescue. But even more than that, the very fabric of reality was at risk of unraveling, and unless they could stop it, the temporal instability could consume everything.

Time was running out—in more ways than one.

Chapter 28: The Lost Crew

The decision had been made: a covert mission would be launched to locate and, if possible, recover the *Challenger* crew from the other side of the dimensional rift. The risk was enormous, the science untested, and the outcome uncertain, but there was no other choice. Time was running out—not only for the crew but for reality itself. The rift, now expanding with terrifying speed, threatened to merge two timelines into one chaotic, unpredictable existence.

Dr. Allan Hayes stood in the operations center at NASA, surrounded by his team and a select group of military and intelligence operatives. The gravity of the situation weighed heavily on everyone. The task before them wasn't just about saving the *Challenger* crew—it was about preventing the collapse of time and space.

"Everyone knows the stakes," Hayes said, addressing the room. "The temporal instability is spreading. If we don't act now, the rift will continue to grow, and we could see a complete convergence of realities. We're sending in a recovery team—this is our one shot."

The mission would be unlike anything ever attempted. The recovery team, composed of both NASA astronauts and military operatives, would be sent into the rift using experimental technology designed to stabilize their connection to the present timeline. They would be equipped with advanced suits capable of withstanding the temporal distortions within the rift, as well as tracking devices linked to the faint signals coming from the *Challenger*. Their objective was simple: locate the shuttle and bring the crew back—if they were still alive.

Eliza Langston, who had been instrumental in developing the stabilization technology, explained the mechanics of the mission. "The rift is a tear in the fabric of space-time," she said, pointing to the holographic display of the anomaly. "We believe that the *Challenger* and its crew are trapped in a pocket of distorted time—an alternate dimension where they're reliving events in a loop. Our goal is to sync the recovery team's temporal signature with the shuttle's and pull them back into our timeline. But the window is narrow. If the rift destabilizes further, they could be lost forever."

Commander Jack Reynolds, a veteran astronaut selected to lead the recovery team, listened intently. "What kind of resistance are we expecting once we enter the rift?"

"We don't know for sure," Hayes admitted. "But based on the temporal anomalies we've observed, you could encounter anything—fragments of the past, future, or alternate realities. Time doesn't behave the way we understand it within the rift. You'll need to rely on the stabilization systems to keep you anchored."

The room fell silent as the weight of the mission settled over the group. They were about to embark on a rescue mission into a place where time itself was broken, and the risks were unlike anything ever faced by space explorers. But this was their only chance to save the crew of the *Challenger*—and perhaps stop the convergence from tearing their world apart.

Hours later, the recovery team stood on the launchpad, suited up and ready. The mission would use a modified space shuttle equipped with experimental technology designed to protect the crew from the temporal distortions. The shuttle itself had been retrofitted with temporal stabilizers, massive generators that would create a bubble of stabilized time around the craft as it entered the rift.

Commander Reynolds, along with the four other members of his team, took their positions inside the shuttle. In addition to Reynolds, the team included Dr. Eliza Langston, who would monitor the temporal stabilization systems, and two military operatives trained in rescue and retrieval operations. The final member of the team was Dana Walker, whose expertise in decoding the *Challenger*'s signals had made her an essential part of the mission.

As the countdown began, the reality of what they were about to attempt settled in. They were heading into the unknown—into a rift that could lead anywhere, to any time. But they were prepared. They had to be.

"Mission control, we are go for launch," Commander Reynolds said, his voice calm despite the tension in the air.

"Roger that, *Discovery*," Hayes replied from mission control, using the name of the shuttle that would carry them into the rift. "Good luck. We're all counting on you."

The engines roared to life, and within moments, the *Discovery* shot into the sky, streaking toward the rift that hovered like a dark, pulsating wound in the atmosphere over Cape Canaveral. As they approached the rift, the familiar sights of Earth below seemed to blur, as though reality itself was bending. The air around them grew thick with an invisible tension, and the temporal stabilizers hummed with power as they activated.

"Entering the rift in T-minus ten seconds," Eliza said, her voice steady but tense. "Stabilizers are holding. Stay sharp, everyone."

The shuttle's nose tilted upward as they breached the edge of the rift. Outside, the sky twisted and warped, as though space and time were folding in on themselves. The stars disappeared, replaced by swirling, disjointed fragments of light and shadow. It was like flying into a fractured mirror—each shard a different version of reality, each reflection a possibility that could have been.

"Temporal distortion increasing," Dana reported, her hands flying across the console as she monitored the signals. "We're picking up the *Challenger*'s signal—it's faint, but it's there."

The team's heart rates spiked as they realized they were getting closer. The *Challenger* was out there, somewhere in the rift, lost between timelines. The shuttle's systems strained to maintain the temporal bubble around them, preventing them from being pulled into the chaos outside.

Suddenly, a warning alarm blared. "We've got an anomaly dead ahead," Reynolds called out. "Brace yourselves!"

Through the front window of the shuttle, they saw it—an impossible sight. The *Challenger*, flickering in and out of existence, its shape distorted by the rift's temporal distortions. The shuttle looked as though it were caught in a loop, phasing between different points in time. Sometimes it appeared whole, the crew inside alive and well, as if preparing for a successful mission. Other times, it was a wreck, the remnants of the explosion frozen in time.

"There they are," Dana whispered, her voice trembling. "The crew."

Through the distortion, they could see the figures of the *Challenger*'s crew, moving in slow motion, unaware of the temporal chaos surrounding them. Commander Francis Scobee was at the helm, his expression calm but confused, as if he were repeating the same actions over and over, trapped in a loop of time that had no end.

"We're going in," Reynolds said, his voice hard as steel. "Hold onto your temporal stabilizers—this is going to be rough."

The *Discovery* moved closer to the *Challenger*, the stabilizers humming louder as they attempted to synchronize the two shuttles' temporal signatures. Inside the rift, the team's senses were assaulted by disorienting flashes of alternate realities—futures that never happened, pasts that had been forgotten. Time bent and twisted around them, and for a moment, it felt like they were everywhere at once.

Eliza worked furiously at her console, trying to establish a stable link between the two shuttles. "We need to sync with their timeline," she said, her voice tight with concentration. "If we can match their temporal signature, we can pull them out."

Dana's hands moved faster than ever, isolating the *Challenger*'s signals and feeding them into the temporal stabilizers. "I've got them," she said, her voice filled with both hope and fear. "We just need a little more time."

The *Discovery* inched closer, and suddenly, the two shuttles aligned. The *Challenger* stabilized, its form becoming clear and solid. The recovery team could see the crew—alive, confused, but there. Commander Scobee looked up, as if finally seeing the rescue shuttle for the first time.

"Francis, this is Reynolds," the commander said through the comms. "We're here to bring you home. Hold on."

But just as the recovery team prepared to lock onto the *Challenger* and pull them out of the rift, the stabilizers began to fluctuate. Alarms blared as the temporal distortion surged.

"The rift is destabilizing!" Eliza shouted. "We're losing them!"

"No!" Dana cried, her hands shaking as she fought to maintain the connection. "We're so close!"

The shuttles began to drift apart, pulled by the forces of the rift as reality itself started to collapse around them. Commander Scobee reached out, as if trying to grasp the rescue team, but his figure began to flicker once more, fading in and out of existence.

"We can't lose them!" Reynolds shouted. "Eliza, do something!"

But before anyone could react, the *Challenger* vanished, pulled back into the depths of the rift, leaving only silence behind.

The mission had failed.

For now, the crew of the *Challenger* remained lost, trapped in a world between worlds, waiting for a rescue that might never come.

But the team knew they couldn't give up. Time was slipping away, both for the *Challenger* and for their reality. They had to find another way to bring them back—before the rift consumed everything.

Chapter 29: The Hidden Agenda

As the failure of the covert rescue mission weighed heavily on Dr. Allan Hayes and his team, a new and darker truth began to emerge. What had originally been dismissed as a tragic accident involving the *Challenger* was now taking on an entirely different dimension—both figuratively and literally. Information began to surface that certain NASA officials and high-ranking government personnel had been aware of the possibility of dimensional anomalies long before the shuttle's ill-fated launch.

For months, Hayes, Eliza Langston, Dana Walker, and the rest of the team had been working tirelessly to understand the rift and the temporal instability surrounding Cape Canaveral. But now, as they dug deeper into classified files and obscure reports, they began to realize they had been chasing an incomplete truth. The disaster that had unfolded on January 28, 1986, was not merely the result of a mechanical failure or even an unexplained phenomenon. It was the product of a deliberate gamble, one made by those in power who had known more than they ever admitted.

It started with a series of leaked documents, brought to Hayes' attention by an anonymous source. The documents, stamped with the highest levels of classification, dated back years before the *Challenger* launch. They contained references to "anomalous energy signatures" and "unexplained dimensional fluctuations" detected during earlier shuttle missions—signals that closely resembled the ones now being picked up from the *Challenger*. These documents suggested that, long before the ill-fated mission, NASA and certain government agencies had been aware of the possibility that space near Earth might not be as stable as they had believed.

Hayes stared at the report in disbelief, his heart pounding. Eliza, standing beside him, leafed through the files, her face growing pale.

"They knew," she whispered, her voice laced with shock and anger. "They knew something was wrong. They detected dimensional anomalies years before the *Challenger* launched."

"They didn't just know," Hayes replied, shaking his head as he struggled to make sense of it. "They were studying it. Testing it. These signatures—they match the same energy spikes we've been tracking near the rift."

It wasn't just a few isolated incidents, either. The documents revealed that several previous shuttle missions had experienced similar anomalies, though none had resulted in a full-scale rift. The data had been quietly swept under the rug, buried deep within classified files that only a select few had access to.

As they continued reading, a chilling pattern began to emerge. A secret group within NASA, working in conjunction with the Department of Defense and other shadowy government entities, had been monitoring these anomalies for years. Codenamed **Project Horizon**, this group had been formed after an incident involving a shuttle test flight in the early 1980s. During that flight, the shuttle had briefly encountered strange gravitational shifts and energy spikes similar to those observed during the *Challenger* mission.

But instead of halting further missions, Project Horizon had seen these anomalies as an opportunity—an unprecedented chance to explore the boundaries of space-time itself.

"They weren't just trying to avoid the anomalies," Dana said, her voice barely above a whisper as she skimmed through the files. "They were trying to harness them."

The implications were staggering. The *Challenger* disaster had not been a random tragedy caused by a faulty O-ring or an unlucky string of events. It had been part of a larger experiment, one designed to push the boundaries of what humanity knew about space-time and dimensional travel. And the crew of the *Challenger*—heroes, astronauts, pioneers—had been unwitting participants in a mission whose true objectives had been hidden from them.

Hayes clenched his fists, rage and frustration building within him. "They sacrificed the crew for this. They knew there was a risk, and they let the mission go ahead anyway."

Eliza nodded, her face set in grim determination. "The dimensional anomalies, the rift, the temporal instability—it all started because they were meddling with forces they didn't understand. And now we're paying the price."

As the team pored over the newly revealed documents, they found more evidence of cover-ups and deliberate manipulation. High-ranking officials at NASA, the Department of Defense, and even certain members of the White House had been briefed on the potential for "dimensional breaches" long before the *Challenger* launch. They had been warned that the anomalies could lead to catastrophic consequences, but those warnings had been ignored—or worse, deliberately suppressed.

One particularly damning memo, written just weeks before the *Challenger* launch, outlined the possibility that the shuttle's mission could intersect with an unstable "dimensional node" near Earth's orbit. The memo, addressed to a group of top-level officials, had been stamped with a chilling note: **"Proceed with caution, but proceed."**

"Proceed with caution?" Dana repeated incredulously, her hands trembling as she held the document. "They knew the risks, and they still went ahead with the launch?"

"They were hoping to prove something," Hayes said darkly. "They thought they could control the anomaly—use it to unlock new frontiers in space travel or even manipulate time itself. But instead, they tore open a rift that they couldn't close."

The revelation that the government had known about the possibility of dimensional anomalies—and had actively pursued their study—changed everything. Project Horizon hadn't just been an experiment; it had been a calculated risk, one that had gone horribly wrong. And now, as the rift continued to expand and the temporal instability threatened to consume everything, the consequences of that risk were becoming all too clear.

Eliza spoke up, her voice filled with a sense of urgency. "We need to expose this. The public needs to know what really happened, what they've been hiding."

But Hayes knew that exposing the truth wouldn't be easy. Project Horizon was classified at the highest levels, and the people behind it had immense power. Even now, they were likely watching, waiting to see how much the team had uncovered. There was no telling what they would do to keep the truth buried.

"We can't just sit on this information," Hayes said, his voice firm. "But we need to be smart. If we come out with this too soon, they'll bury us—just like they buried the evidence of the anomalies. We need more proof, more allies."

Dana nodded. "We still have people inside NASA who don't know the full story. We can reach out to them—get them on our side before we make our move."

Eliza glanced at the map of the rift's expansion on the screen, her expression hardening. "But we can't wait too long. The rift is growing. The convergence is accelerating. If we don't stop it soon, none of this will matter."

As the team prepared to launch the next phase of their plan, they knew they were walking a dangerous line. The truth about Project Horizon and the hidden agenda behind the *Challenger* mission could bring down some of the most powerful people in the government, but it could also save the world from the disaster that was now unfolding.

Time was running out—both for the truth to be revealed and for the rift to be closed. And as Hayes and his team prepared to confront the forces behind Project Horizon, they knew they were about to face their greatest challenge yet.

The stakes were no longer just about the past or the future. They were about the very fabric of reality itself.

Chapter 30: Warnings from the Beyond

As the rift continued to expand and reality itself teetered on the edge of collapse, NASA's communications experts began picking up strange, urgent signals that no one could explain. These transmissions were garbled, fragmented by interference from the dimensional anomaly, but they carried an unmistakable sense of warning—messages from the other side of the rift, perhaps even from the *Challenger* crew that had survived in an alternate dimension.

At first, the signals were dismissed as more interference caused by the growing temporal instability around Cape Canaveral. But as the communications team dug deeper into the data, they began to notice a pattern. The signals were not random noise; they were deliberate. Someone—or something—was trying to make contact, to send a message through the chaos of the rift. And the messages were growing more urgent with each passing day.

In the communications lab, Dana Walker and a team of experts worked around the clock, analyzing every scrap of data they could intercept. The signals were weak, distorted by the dimensional rift, but beneath the static, they could hear voices. Dana leaned closer to her console, adjusting the frequency as the voices crackled through her headphones.

"This is... Scobee. Commander Scobee of the *Challenger*. Can anyone...?"

Her heart skipped a beat. It was unmistakable—the voice of Commander Francis Scobee, the man who had been lost along with his crew when the *Challenger* exploded. But this transmission wasn't a relic from the past; it was coming through in real-time, from the other side of the rift.

"Francis, do you copy?" Dana said urgently into her microphone, her hands shaking as she tried to lock onto the signal. "This is Dana Walker. We hear you."

The signal wavered, dipping in and out of existence, but Scobee's voice broke through again, more fragmented than before.

"...Can't hold... something's wrong... reality... collapsing... convergence..."

Dana's stomach turned as the words sank in. The messages weren't just from a stranded crew—they were warnings. Scobee's voice faded out, replaced by static, but not before one final message came through, clear and desperate:

"...Stop the convergence... before it's too late."

The room fell silent as Dana processed what she had just heard. She immediately flagged the transmission and sent it to Dr. Allan Hayes and Eliza Langston, who had been following the anomalies closely. Within minutes, they arrived in the communications lab, tension etched into their faces.

"You heard it?" Hayes asked, his voice tight with urgency.

Dana nodded. "It was Scobee. I'm sure of it. He's out there, in the rift, and he's warning us. He said we have to stop the convergence, or reality will collapse."

Eliza's face was pale as she stared at the waveform on the screen. "This isn't just about saving the crew anymore. If the convergence continues, it will destroy both dimensions. We're running out of time."

Hayes rubbed his temples, his mind racing. The warnings from the other side of the rift confirmed their worst fears: the convergence wasn't just a temporal anomaly—it was a full-scale collapse of reality, and it was accelerating. The dimensional boundaries were breaking down, and soon, the two worlds would be irrevocably merged, with catastrophic consequences.

But the messages also brought a glimmer of hope. The *Challenger* crew was still alive—at least, in some form. They were trapped in the alternate dimension, but they were aware of what was happening, and they were trying to help. If they could communicate through the rift, there was still a chance to stop the convergence.

"Can we respond to them?" Hayes asked, turning to Dana. "Can we send a message back through the rift?"

"We're working on it," Dana replied. "But the interference is getting worse. The rift is distorting everything. It's like trying to send a message through a broken mirror."

Hayes looked over at Eliza, his expression grim. "We need to figure out how to stop the convergence—and fast. If the crew can see what's happening from their side, they might know more about how the rift works. We need to find a way to communicate with them."

Eliza nodded, her mind already racing through possible solutions. "We could try stabilizing the signal with a temporal anchor. If we can synchronize our timeline with theirs, even for a few minutes, we might be able to get a clear transmission."

Dana's hands flew over the controls as she worked to boost the signal. "I'll do everything I can. But we're running out of time. The rift is getting worse by the hour."

As the team worked frantically to strengthen the connection, more transmissions began to come through—some from Commander Scobee, others from the rest of the *Challenger* crew. The messages were broken, filled with fragments of warnings and descriptions of what they were experiencing on the other side.

"This is... Ronald McNair... we're caught in a loop... can't find a way out..."

"...Reality is... splintering... time doesn't work the same here... each time we try to escape, we end up back where we started..."

"...We're seeing... echoes of other versions of ourselves... like we're stuck between timelines..."

The voices were haunting, filled with fear and confusion. It was clear that the crew was trapped in a place where time and space no longer followed the rules they had once understood. The rift had pulled them into a liminal space, a reality between realities, and they were desperate to find a way back.

But the most chilling message came from Christa McAuliffe, the schoolteacher who had been aboard the *Challenger* as part of NASA's Teacher in Space Program. Her voice, calm but filled with an eerie certainty, cut through the static.

"We've seen what happens if the rift isn't closed," McAuliffe said. "The convergence—it doesn't just merge two worlds. It destroys them. We've lived through it, in different timelines. Each time, it ends the same. If you don't stop it, both realities will collapse into nothingness."

The team listened in stunned silence. The warnings weren't just theoretical—they were based on lived experiences. The crew had been trapped in the rift for what felt like an eternity, reliving the same catastrophic outcomes over and over again, caught in a loop of failed timelines. Each time, the convergence had destroyed everything.

"Christa, this is Hayes," Allan said, his voice filled with urgency as he leaned into the microphone. "We're trying to stop the convergence, but we need to know how. What can we do?"

There was a long pause, filled with the crackling of static. When McAuliffe's voice returned, it was faint, but resolute.

"You have to close the rift from both sides," she said. "We've been trying to shut it down from here, but we need your help. The rift is anchored to the moment of the explosion. If you can stabilize the point of divergence—where our realities split—you can prevent the convergence."

Eliza's eyes widened as she realized what McAuliffe was saying. "The explosion wasn't just an accident," she whispered. "It was the moment the two dimensions began to bleed into each other. If we can stabilize that point in time, we might be able to close the rift and stop the collapse."

Dana's hands flew across the controls as she adjusted the signal, trying to keep the connection stable. "But how do we do that? The explosion is in the past."

"It's not just in the past," Eliza replied, her mind working furiously. "It's part of the rift. The explosion is still happening, in a way—trapped in the loop of the convergence. We need to find a way to manipulate the timeline, to anchor both realities to a stable point."

Hayes nodded, his expression grim but determined. "We'll figure it out. But first, we need to strengthen our connection to the crew. They're our only link to the other side."

As the team worked to stabilize the communication link, the voices of the *Challenger* crew grew more faint, as if they were slipping further away into the rift.

"We don't have much time," McAuliffe said, her voice barely audible through the interference. "If the convergence reaches critical mass, there won't be anything left to save. You have to stop it... before it's too late."

And with that, the signal went dead, leaving only silence behind.

The warnings from the beyond had been heard. Now, it was up to Hayes, Eliza, Dana, and the rest of the team to find a way to stop the convergence and save not just the *Challenger* crew, but both realities from total collapse.

Time was running out, and the fate of two worlds hung in the balance.

Chapter 31: The Rescue Mission

The weight of the messages from the *Challenger* crew hung over the NASA control room like a heavy cloud. The warnings from the alternate dimension had made it clear: time was running out. The convergence between the two realities was accelerating, and if it wasn't stopped, both worlds would collapse into nothingness. There was only one option left: to launch a rescue mission into the dimensional rift. It was the most dangerous mission ever conceived, but it had to be done. The fate of both realities—and the lost *Challenger* crew—depended on it.

Dr. Allan Hayes, Eliza Langston, Dana Walker, and the rest of the team stood around the holographic display, reviewing the details of the mission. The rift was expanding rapidly, its energy signatures growing more erratic with each passing hour. The window to save the crew and stop the convergence was closing fast.

"We've received the warnings loud and clear," Hayes said, his voice steady despite the tension in the room. "The crew of the *Challenger* is trapped in an alternate dimension, and they've been trying to close the rift from their side. But they can't do it alone. If we don't stabilize the point of divergence—the moment of the explosion—both realities will collapse."

Commander Jack Reynolds, who had led the previous covert mission, was once again selected to spearhead the operation. He stood at the front of the room, wearing his modified flight suit, his expression hard but focused. This time, the stakes were even higher.

"We're going back in," Reynolds said, his voice filled with grim determination. "Our mission is twofold: rescue the *Challenger* crew and, if possible, close the rift from inside. If we can't pull them out, we'll have to seal the rift to stop the convergence."

The room was silent as everyone absorbed the enormity of the task before them. Entering the rift was a journey into the unknown, a leap into a dimension where time and space no longer followed the rules. The team would have to navigate a reality where the past, present, and future collided, all while trying to stabilize the temporal anomaly that had torn open the rift in the first place.

Eliza Langston took the floor next, explaining the technology they would use for the mission. "We've made upgrades to the temporal stabilizers based on the data we've collected from the rift. This time, we're equipping the shuttle with a quantum resonance drive. It should allow us to anchor the shuttle to both realities and synchronize with the temporal signature of the *Challenger* crew. Once inside the rift, we'll use the drive to lock onto the point of divergence and close the tear in space-time."

The team listened intently, but the tension in the air was palpable. The mission was fraught with risks. The rift had become highly unstable, and any miscalculation could mean disaster—not just for the crew inside, but for both realities.

Commander Reynolds turned to Dana, who had played a key role in establishing communication with the *Challenger* crew. "Dana, we're going to need you with us again. You're the best chance we have at maintaining a link with the crew once we're inside."

Dana nodded, her face determined but anxious. "I'll be ready. We've fine-tuned the communications array, so we should be able to maintain a link longer this time. But once we're in the rift, anything could happen."

The plan was simple in theory but perilous in execution. The shuttle, once inside the rift, would have to navigate through the dimensional turbulence, find the *Challenger*, and attempt to synchronize the two timelines. If successful, they would either bring the crew back or close the rift entirely, preventing the convergence from reaching critical mass.

As the final preparations were made, the gravity of the mission weighed heavily on everyone involved. The *Challenger* crew had been trapped in a fractured reality for what felt like an eternity. They had witnessed the collapse of their world over and over, sending desperate messages through the rift in a last-ditch effort to save both dimensions. Now, it was up to this new crew to enter the rift and finish what the *Challenger* had started.

On the launchpad, the *Endeavour*, a shuttle retrofitted with experimental technology, stood ready. Its exterior gleamed under the lights of the Cape Canaveral launch facility, its modifications barely visible but crucial to the mission's success. The shuttle was equipped with temporal stabilizers, quantum field generators, and communication arrays designed to maintain contact with the *Challenger* once inside the rift.

Commander Reynolds, Dana Walker, and the rest of the mission team boarded the shuttle, each member acutely aware of the stakes. Eliza Langston and Dr. Allan Hayes remained in mission control, their eyes glued to the monitors as the countdown began.

"T-minus 10 seconds," the launch director announced over the intercom.

Inside the *Endeavour*, the crew felt the familiar rumble as the engines powered up. Outside, the sky was dark, lit only by the shuttle's blazing engines and the ominous, swirling mass of the rift hovering above Cape Canaveral.

"T-minus 5 seconds."

Reynolds gripped the controls, his jaw set. This was it—their chance to stop the convergence, to save the *Challenger* crew, and perhaps even reality itself.

"3... 2... 1... Liftoff!"

The *Endeavour* roared into the sky, leaving the Earth behind as it hurtled toward the rift. The shuttle pierced through the atmosphere, the stars above them warping as they neared the dimensional tear. The temporal stabilizers hummed to life, creating a protective bubble around the shuttle as it approached the swirling vortex of the rift.

"We're approaching the rift," Reynolds said, his voice steady over the comms. "Stabilizers are holding. Everyone, brace yourselves. This is where things get weird."

As the *Endeavour* entered the rift, the view outside the shuttle became a kaleidoscope of shifting realities. Time and space bent around them, folding and distorting as fragments of alternate timelines collided. The shuttle shook violently as it passed through layers of temporal energy, each pulse sending ripples through the fabric of reality.

"Hold it steady!" Dana called out, her hands flying across the console as she monitored the communications link. "I'm picking up the *Challenger*'s signal. They're close."

Reynolds adjusted the controls, guiding the shuttle deeper into the rift. Outside the window, they caught glimpses of alternate versions of Earth—some familiar, others impossibly alien. The past and future blurred together, with images of the *Challenger* shuttle flickering in and out of existence, caught in an endless loop.

"There!" Dana shouted, her voice filled with hope. "I've got them. The *Challenger* is ahead."

Through the distortion, they saw it—the *Challenger*, hovering in the distance, caught in the swirling chaos of the rift. The shuttle was phasing in and out, its crew visible for brief moments before vanishing again. It was as if they were suspended in time, trapped between realities.

Reynolds brought the *Endeavour* closer, the stabilizers working overtime to synchronize with the *Challenger*'s temporal signature.

"Commander Scobee, do you copy?" Dana said into the comms, her voice tense with urgency.

For a long moment, there was nothing but static. Then, through the interference, Scobee's voice came through—faint, but alive.

"This is Scobee. We're here... trapped... can't break the loop. You have to help us."

"We're locking onto your position," Reynolds replied, guiding the shuttle closer to the *Challenger*. "Hold on, we're going to pull you out."

As the two shuttles aligned, Eliza Langston's voice came over the comms from mission control. "You're almost there. Synchronize the temporal signatures and initiate the quantum resonance drive. That should anchor both shuttles to our timeline."

Dana worked furiously at the console, adjusting the frequencies until the two shuttles were in perfect sync. "We've got them," she said, her voice filled with relief. "Initiating the quantum resonance drive."

The shuttle shook violently as the drive activated, creating a surge of energy that rippled through the rift. Outside, the swirling chaos began to stabilize, the fractured timelines slowing as the two realities synchronized.

"We're pulling them out," Reynolds said, his hands steady on the controls. "Stay with us, *Challenger*."

But just as the shuttles began to merge, the rift pulsed violently, sending a shockwave through both crafts. Alarms blared inside the *Endeavour* as the temporal stabilizers struggled to maintain their hold.

"The rift is destabilizing!" Dana shouted. "We're losing them!"

"No!" Reynolds shouted, fighting to keep control of the shuttle. "We can't lose them now!"

But the forces of the rift were too strong. In a final, desperate moment, the *Challenger* began to flicker, its form dissolving into the swirling vortex. The crew's voices echoed through the comms one last time before fading into silence.

And then, the *Challenger* was gone.

The *Endeavour* emerged from the rift, the mission incomplete. The crew had failed to rescue the *Challenger*, but the rift was stabilizing. The convergence had been stopped—at least for now.

In the aftermath, the team back at NASA was left with a bittersweet victory. The *Challenger* crew remained lost in the alternate dimension, but their warnings had saved both realities. The rift was closing, but at a great cost.

For Hayes, Dana, Eliza, and Reynolds, the mission was far from over. There was still hope—however faint—that they might find a way to bring the *Challenger* crew home. But for now, they had bought time, and the world was safe from the collapse of space-time.

The *Challenger* had been lost, but its legacy—and its crew—would never be forgotten.

Chapter 32: The Alternate Earth

The *Endeavour* had returned safely to Earth, but the failure to rescue the *Challenger* crew weighed heavily on the team. Though they had stabilized the rift and temporarily halted the convergence, they knew their mission wasn't over. The crew of the *Challenger* was still out there, lost in an alternate dimension. And now, with the lessons they'd learned from the first mission, NASA and the team were ready to take one last, desperate gamble—a mission directly into the alternate dimension to bring the *Challenger* crew back or, if that failed, to learn more about the world on the other side.

Dr. Allan Hayes, Eliza Langston, Commander Jack Reynolds, Dana Walker, and the rest of the mission team gathered in NASA's operations center once again, the atmosphere tense with anticipation. This time, they had a new objective: to go beyond the rift and explore the alternate dimension where the *Challenger* had been trapped.

"We've received fragmented signals from the *Challenger* crew," Hayes said, his voice steady but filled with urgency. "They've been trying to communicate with us, sending warnings about a convergence. But we've also picked up something else—glimpses of a world that looks like ours but... different. There's something about this other Earth that we need to understand."

Eliza stood next to Hayes, outlining the mission parameters. "We're launching a second shuttle into the rift, but this time we'll go deeper. We're not just looking for the *Challenger*—we're looking to understand the nature of the alternate dimension. From what we've gathered, the Earth on the other side is fundamentally different. History took another path, and we need to figure out what that means for the convergence."

Commander Jack Reynolds nodded, his expression grim. He would once again lead the team into the unknown, this time with a clearer picture of what they were up against. The temporal stabilizers had been upgraded, and the shuttle had been outfitted with advanced quantum sensors to map the alternate dimension and gather data on its energy signatures. This wasn't just a rescue mission anymore—it was an exploration of another reality.

As the *Endeavour* prepared for launch, the crew knew this mission would be their most dangerous yet. The rift had stabilized, but there was no guarantee that it would stay that way. And the alternate dimension they were about to enter had already proven to be unpredictable, filled with dangers they couldn't fully understand.

"T-minus 10 seconds," the launch director called out, as the *Endeavour* stood poised on the launchpad once more.

Commander Reynolds and his crew braced themselves as the engines roared to life, propelling the shuttle skyward. Within moments, they breached the atmosphere, heading directly toward the rift. The familiar distortion of space and time greeted them as they entered the swirling vortex, the temporal stabilizers humming as they worked to keep the shuttle anchored to their timeline.

"This is it," Reynolds said, his hands steady on the controls. "We're entering the alternate dimension."

As the shuttle passed through the rift, the view outside shifted. The kaleidoscope of fractured realities faded, and suddenly, the crew found themselves looking down at a planet that looked remarkably like Earth—but with subtle, unnerving differences.

"Is that... Earth?" Dana whispered, her eyes wide as she gazed out the window.

It was Earth, but not their Earth. The planet's continents were the same, the oceans familiar, but the landscape below told a different story. Massive cities sprawled across vast stretches of land, far larger and denser than those on their Earth. Strange, towering structures dotted the landscape, gleaming with unfamiliar technology. And in the skies above, a fleet of advanced aircraft patrolled the skies, their designs sleek and angular, unlike anything they had seen before.

"We're in the alternate dimension," Eliza said, her voice filled with awe and trepidation. "This is what the *Challenger* crew was warning us about. We need to gather as much data as we can."

Reynolds guided the *Endeavour* into low orbit as the quantum sensors began mapping the planet's surface. The data pouring in confirmed their suspicions—this Earth was similar to their own, but history had taken a different path.

"We're picking up strange energy signatures across the planet," Dana said, her hands flying across the console. "It's like the entire Earth is powered by some kind of advanced fusion technology. But it's more than that—there's an underlying instability in the atmosphere, like the planet is constantly on the edge of some kind of collapse."

Eliza's eyes narrowed as she examined the readings. "It's the convergence. This world is experiencing its own form of instability, just like ours. The dimensional rift isn't just affecting our Earth—it's affecting this one too."

As they continued their observations, they began to pick up transmissions from the planet below. The language was recognizable, but the content sent chills down their spines.

"The Cold War," Dana said, her voice shaking as she listened to the broadcasts. "It never ended."

The transmissions revealed a world still locked in a decades-long standoff between two superpowers—the United States and the Soviet Union. But unlike the Cold War that had ended in their reality, this conflict had continued unabated. Both nations had developed terrifying new technologies, fueled by the same dimensional anomalies that had created the rift in the first place. The arms race had spiraled out of control, with each side stockpiling weapons capable of devastating entire cities—and possibly the planet itself.

"This is why the *Challenger* crew warned us," Hayes said, his voice low. "This Earth is on the brink of destruction. The Cold War never ended, and now both realities are facing collapse because of the rift."

The team's mission had just become even more urgent. The convergence wasn't just threatening their world—it was destabilizing the alternate Earth as well. If they didn't find a way to close the rift, both realities would be consumed in the chaos.

"We need to make contact," Reynolds said, his voice firm. "If the *Challenger* crew is down there, they might be our only chance of figuring out how to stop this."

As the *Endeavour* descended through the atmosphere, the crew prepared for the next phase of their mission: a landing on the alternate Earth. The air outside shimmered with energy as the temporal stabilizers strained to hold the shuttle's position in the unstable dimension. Below them, the cities grew larger, the scale of the Cold War-era infrastructure more imposing with each passing moment.

As they approached the surface, the shuttle's sensors picked up signs of advanced military installations, including vast underground bunkers and missile silos. The tension was palpable—this was a world on the verge of total war, one spark away from global catastrophe.

The *Endeavour* touched down in a remote area outside one of the massive cities. The crew disembarked, their suits equipped with temporal shielding to protect them from the dimension's instability. As they stepped onto the surface of the alternate Earth, they felt the strange, disorienting pull of the rift, a reminder that they were walking on the edge of two realities.

"We've picked up the *Challenger*'s signal," Dana said, her voice filled with hope. "It's faint, but it's coming from somewhere nearby."

The crew moved cautiously through the eerie landscape, the city looming in the distance. As they followed the signal, they began to encounter signs of life—people who looked just like those from their Earth, but whose expressions were hardened by decades of conflict. Military patrols roamed the streets, their eyes scanning the skies for signs of enemy activity.

"This is a world preparing for war," Eliza said quietly, her heart heavy. "They're on the brink of annihilation."

As the team reached the source of the signal, they found themselves standing in front of an abandoned facility—an old launch complex, long since forgotten in their reality but still intact here. And inside, they made a shocking discovery.

The *Challenger* crew was there—alive, but changed.

Commander Francis Scobee, Ronald McNair, Christa McAuliffe, and the rest of the crew had survived the rift, but they had been living in this alternate dimension for what felt like years. Time had passed differently here, and the crew had aged, their faces marked by the hardships they had endured.

"We tried to warn you," Scobee said, his voice filled with both relief and sorrow as he saw the rescue team. "This world is collapsing, just like ours. The convergence is happening faster than we thought. If we don't stop it, both Earths will be destroyed."

The crew's warnings had been true all along. The alternate Earth was a reflection of what could have been—a world where conflict and paranoia had persisted, and where the consequences of the rift were being felt just as acutely.

"We're not leaving without you," Reynolds said firmly. "But we need your help. How do we close the rift?"

Scobee nodded, his expression grim but determined. "We need to stabilize both sides of the rift. It's the only way to stop the convergence."

As the team prepared to execute the final phase of their mission, they knew that time was running out. The fate of both Earths now rested on their ability to work together, to bridge the gap between dimensions and close the tear in space-time once and for all.

But as they worked, they couldn't help but wonder: was the price of saving their world worth leaving this alternate Earth to its own destruction?

The clock was ticking, and the final confrontation with the rift was about to begin.

Chapter 33: The Return of the Challenger

The moment Commander Jack Reynolds and his team stepped into the derelict launch complex, it felt like they had crossed into a dream—or perhaps a nightmare. The complex was eerily familiar yet alien in its design, a relic from a world that had diverged from their own decades ago. The team moved cautiously through the corridors, following the faint signal that had brought them here.

And then they found them.

The crew of the *Challenger*, who had been presumed lost in the explosion all those years ago, stood before them—alive, but profoundly changed. Commander Francis Scobee, Ronald McNair, Christa McAuliffe, and the others were there, their faces worn with age and experience, eyes filled with a mix of recognition and disbelief.

Reynolds, Dana Walker, and the rest of the rescue team stared at the *Challenger* crew in awe. They had survived, not just the explosion but years spent trapped in this alternate dimension, living in a world that was both familiar and profoundly different. Time had passed differently here—what had been mere months back on Earth had felt like years for the crew. They had lived through countless struggles, adapting to a reality that was at once recognizable yet fundamentally altered by the continued Cold War tensions and advanced technologies that defined this Earth.

"Commander Scobee," Reynolds said, his voice filled with disbelief. "It's really you."

Scobee stepped forward, his face lined with the weight of the years spent in this world. His once crisp NASA flight suit was worn and faded, a reminder of how long he and his crew had been stranded. Yet, despite the hardship, there was strength in his gaze.

"It's us," Scobee said, his voice steady but somber. "But we've been here far longer than we ever imagined. When we first crossed into the rift, we thought we'd find a way home quickly. But the longer we stayed, the more we realized we were trapped."

Dana took a tentative step forward, her eyes searching the faces of the *Challenger* crew. Christa McAuliffe, once the symbol of hope and inspiration as the first teacher in space, stood beside Scobee. Her eyes, though older and more weary, still held the spark of determination that had carried her through those early days of training. But now, there was something else—a deep sadness born from witnessing the collapse of two worlds.

"We tried to send messages," McAuliffe said quietly, her voice carrying the weight of years of struggle. "At first, we thought maybe it was just a technical issue—something with the shuttle or the atmosphere of this world. But as time went on, we realized it was something far worse. We weren't just stranded. We were living in a fractured reality."

The rescue team gathered around, listening in silence as the *Challenger* crew recounted their harrowing journey. When the explosion had occurred, it had torn the shuttle from their timeline, flinging them into this alternate Earth where history had taken a darker turn. The Cold War had never ended, and both the United States and the Soviet Union had built towering empires of technology and weaponry, locked in a never-ending standoff.

"We were taken in by this world's NASA," Scobee explained. "At first, they thought we were from their Earth, some secret experiment that had gone wrong. But it didn't take long for them to realize we were from another dimension. They tried to help us find a way back, but their technology was far behind what we needed. Over time, we became part of this world, watching as it slowly fell apart."

The rescue team stood in stunned silence, trying to process what they were hearing. The *Challenger* crew had lived through years of conflict in this alternate Earth, witnessing the slow decay of a society gripped by fear and paranoia, where advanced technology had not brought peace but only extended the Cold War into an endless stalemate.

Commander Reynolds cleared his throat, breaking the silence. "We're here to bring you home. We've stabilized the rift, and with your help, we can close it. But we need to act fast—the convergence between our worlds is accelerating. If we don't stop it, both realities will collapse."

Scobee nodded, his expression grim. "We know. We've seen it happen—over and over, in different timelines. The rift is like a wound in the fabric of reality, and if we don't close it from both sides, neither world will survive."

Christa McAuliffe stepped forward, her voice soft but resolute. "We've spent years trying to figure out how to stop the convergence, but we couldn't do it alone. Now that you're here, we have a chance."

As the two crews—one from the present and one from the past—came together, the weight of their mission settled on everyone's shoulders. This was their only chance to save both worlds. But the *Challenger* crew had been changed by their time in the alternate dimension, their understanding of the rift and the forces at play far more advanced than what anyone on the rescue team could have imagined.

"There's something you need to know," Ronald McNair said, stepping forward. His face, like the others, bore the signs of a hard life lived in the alternate Earth, but his eyes were sharp with intelligence. "The rift isn't just a random anomaly. It's been growing because both worlds are destabilizing each other. When we first arrived here, the rift was small, almost imperceptible. But over the years, as the Cold War continued and this world's technologies became more advanced, the dimensional fabric started to weaken."

The rescue team exchanged uneasy glances. The implications were terrifying—this alternate Earth, with its unchecked technological advancements and military build-up, was directly contributing to the rift's expansion. And if they didn't find a way to stop it, the rift would consume both dimensions.

Commander Reynolds took a deep breath. "So what's the plan? How do we close the rift and stop the convergence?"

Scobee glanced at his crew, then back at Reynolds. "We need to return to the original point of divergence—the moment of the explosion. The rift is anchored to that event, and it's been spreading ever since. If we can get to the source, we might be able to close it."

Eliza Langston, who had been listening intently, spoke up. "We've identified the temporal coordinates of the explosion on our side. If we can synchronize our timelines and stabilize the rift at that point, we might be able to collapse it, sealing the tear between dimensions."

McNair nodded. "Exactly. But it's not just a matter of collapsing the rift—we have to make sure the energy released doesn't trigger another convergence. It has to be done carefully, or we'll just create another tear."

Reynolds looked at his crew, then back at the *Challenger* team. "We've got the technology to do it. But we're going to need all of you to make this work."

Scobee, McAuliffe, and the rest of the *Challenger* crew exchanged glances. They had been waiting for this moment for years—a chance to go home. But they knew the risks.

"We'll do whatever it takes," Scobee said, his voice filled with quiet determination. "We've lived through this world's nightmare long enough. It's time to end it."

With the plan in place, the two crews prepared for the final phase of their mission. Together, they would return to the source of the rift, stabilize the temporal anomaly, and close the tear between dimensions. It was their last chance to save both worlds—and themselves.

As the *Challenger* crew boarded the *Endeavour*, they looked back one last time at the alternate Earth they had called home for so long. It was a world scarred by conflict and fear, but it had also shown them the resilience of the human spirit. Now, they would take that strength with them as they returned to their own world, ready to face whatever came next.

The mission was clear: return the *Challenger* and its crew to their rightful place, and close the rift once and for all. But as they prepared to leave the alternate dimension, there was one final question that lingered in everyone's mind.

Would they truly be able to stop the convergence in time—or was the collapse of both worlds inevitable?

Chapter 34: The Second Explosion

The *Endeavour* ascended from the alternate Earth, its engines humming as it pushed through the thick atmosphere of a world unlike any the crew had ever known. Behind them, the sprawling cities and Cold War-era military infrastructure of a planet trapped in an unending cycle of conflict faded into the distance. But the real danger lay ahead—the rift, still unstable, still growing, anchored to the moment of the *Challenger*'s original explosion.

The rescue team and the surviving *Challenger* crew were united in their mission: to return to the moment of divergence, the point in time when both realities split. If they could stabilize the rift and close it, they could prevent the complete collapse of both dimensions. But as they approached the rift, the ship's instruments began picking up something far more disturbing—a new energy surge, stronger and more volatile than anything they had detected before.

"Commander, we're picking up massive energy fluctuations coming from the rift," Dana Walker said, her hands flying across the console as she tried to make sense of the readings. "It's like the rift is building toward another event—another explosion."

"How bad are we talking?" Reynolds asked, his voice calm but laced with concern.

"Bad," Dana replied. "If these readings are accurate, the energy being released could be catastrophic. We could be looking at an event bigger than the original explosion. If it goes off, it'll rip through both realities, destroying everything."

Commander Francis Scobee, now sitting beside Reynolds in the cockpit, leaned forward, his eyes narrowing as he studied the data. "This is it," he said quietly. "The second explosion. We always knew it was coming."

Reynolds turned to him. "What do you mean?"

Scobee's expression was grim. "The rift is tethered to the moment of the *Challenger* explosion, but it's not a one-time event. The energy from the initial blast created a fracture between dimensions, but the rift has been building toward something bigger ever since. A second explosion—one that could destroy both realities."

Christa McAuliffe, who had been standing nearby, stepped forward. "We've seen glimpses of it, while we were trapped in the alternate dimension. It's like a ticking time bomb, and every time the rift grows, the clock gets closer to zero. If we don't stop it, the convergence will trigger the second explosion. And this time, there won't be anything left."

Reynolds clenched his fists, the weight of their mission growing heavier with each passing moment. "We need to get to the point of divergence—now."

The *Endeavour* pushed deeper into the rift, the surrounding space growing more distorted and chaotic as they neared the temporal epicenter. Outside the shuttle, the familiar sights of fragmented timelines and alternate realities swirled together, merging into a chaotic blur of light and darkness. Time and space were collapsing, folding in on themselves as the convergence accelerated.

"How much time do we have?" Reynolds asked, his hands steady on the controls.

"Minutes, maybe," Eliza Langston replied, her voice tight with urgency as she monitored the temporal stabilizers. "The second explosion is imminent. We need to synchronize the timelines and close the rift before the energy reaches critical mass."

Dana's console began to flash with warnings as the energy spikes intensified. "I'm detecting massive spikes in temporal energy. It's destabilizing faster than we expected."

"Prepare the quantum resonance drive," Reynolds ordered. "We're going to lock onto the point of divergence and stabilize the timeline."

As the *Endeavour* approached the heart of the rift, the moment of the *Challenger* explosion appeared before them—a frozen instant in time, suspended between dimensions. The shuttle hovered just above the wreckage, its form flickering in and out of existence as the timeline fluctuated. It was a haunting sight, the remnants of the explosion still burning in the fractured space between worlds.

"There it is," Scobee said, his voice filled with a mix of dread and determination. "The moment everything went wrong."

The crew worked quickly, aligning the shuttle's temporal stabilizers with the energy signature of the explosion. The quantum resonance drive hummed to life, sending ripples of energy through the rift as they prepared to anchor the timelines together.

"We're in position," Eliza announced. "Synchronizing the timelines... now."

The shuttle shook violently as the resonance drive activated, locking onto the moment of the *Challenger* explosion. The rift began to pulse, its chaotic energy spiraling inward as the timelines started to align. But just as they were about to stabilize the anomaly, a massive shockwave ripped through the shuttle.

"Brace for impact!" Reynolds shouted as the shuttle lurched sideways, alarms blaring.

The second explosion had begun.

Outside the shuttle, the space around the rift warped and twisted, the energy of the explosion tearing through the fabric of reality. The timelines began to fracture, sending shockwaves through both dimensions. The rift, once a tear between two worlds, was now a gaping wound, expanding rapidly as the explosion threatened to consume everything in its path.

"We're losing stability!" Dana shouted, her voice filled with panic as the console flashed with red warnings. "The second explosion is tearing the rift apart!"

Scobee gripped the edge of his seat, his face grim. "We have to stop it. If the explosion completes, both realities are finished."

Eliza worked furiously at her station, her fingers flying across the controls. "We need to reverse the energy flow! If we can collapse the rift before the explosion reaches critical mass, we might be able to contain it."

Reynolds nodded, his jaw clenched. "Do it."

Eliza initiated the sequence, redirecting the energy from the resonance drive back into the rift. The shuttle shook violently as the stabilizers struggled to contain the massive energy surge. Outside, the rift began to shrink, the explosion collapsing inward as the timelines started to realign.

"We're close," Eliza said, her voice tight with concentration. "Just a few more seconds..."

The rift pulsed again, sending another shockwave through the shuttle. The crew gripped their seats as the world around them blurred, time and space warping together as the convergence reached its peak. The explosion was still building, the energy swirling like a storm, threatening to tear both realities apart.

And then, suddenly, it stopped.

The shuttle fell silent as the rift began to stabilize, its chaotic energy fading into a soft, pulsing glow. The second explosion had been averted, the energy contained before it could reach critical mass.

"We did it," Reynolds said, his voice filled with disbelief. "We stopped the explosion."

The crew let out a collective sigh of relief as the shuttle settled back into normal space. Outside, the rift had shrunk to a fraction of its original size, the tear in space-time nearly sealed.

But there was no time for celebration.

"The rift is stabilizing, but we need to close it completely," Scobee said, his voice steady. "If we don't, this will all happen again."

Reynolds turned to Eliza. "How much longer do we need?"

"Just a few more minutes," Eliza replied, her hands moving swiftly over the controls. "We're almost there."

As the team worked to close the rift, the *Challenger* crew sat quietly, watching the remnants of their disaster slowly fade away. They had been caught in the rift for years, living through its horrors, and now they were finally seeing it come to an end.

"The second explosion almost took everything," McAuliffe said softly, her eyes fixed on the fading light of the rift. "But we stopped it. We stopped the convergence."

And as the last of the rift sealed, the crew knew they had succeeded. The tear between dimensions was closed, and the threat of the second explosion had been averted.

Both worlds were safe—at least, for now.

The *Endeavour* had barely escaped the shockwave of the second explosion, but the crew knew their mission wasn't over. Though they had managed to contain the massive energy surge, the rift had left both realities dangerously unstable. The timelines between the two worlds were still out of sync, and they were beginning to merge in unpredictable, chaotic ways. The real nightmare was only just beginning—a race against time to stop the two realities from spiraling into one catastrophic existence.

Dr. Allan Hayes, Eliza Langston, Commander Jack Reynolds, and the *Challenger* crew had stabilized the rift, but it had come at a price. The fragile balance between the two dimensions had been shattered, and now both Earths were on a collision course with one another. The boundaries between the two realities were blurring, causing strange anomalies to appear in both worlds. Objects, people, and entire locations were shifting between dimensions, creating a terrifying mosaic of fragmented timelines.

As the *Endeavour* flew through the remnants of the rift, the view outside was a dizzying display of crossed realities—skylines from both worlds blending together, flashes of alternate versions of Earth bleeding into one another. The crew watched in horror as they witnessed cities from their Earth flickering alongside military installations from the Cold War-ravaged alternate world.

Dana Walker sat at her console, her fingers moving swiftly as she analyzed the growing anomalies. "We've got major timeline disruptions in both dimensions," she said, her voice tight with urgency. "I'm picking up reports of entire buildings disappearing and reappearing on the other side. People are being pulled between realities, and the timelines are collapsing."

Commander Reynolds gripped the controls, guiding the shuttle as best he could through the shifting, unstable space. "We've got to stop this. If the timelines fully merge, we're looking at a complete collapse of both worlds."

Hayes nodded, his face pale as he reviewed the data. "The convergence is happening faster than we expected. Both Earths are starting to overlap in space-time, and the resulting chaos is causing fractures in reality. If we don't find a way to stop it, both universes will be torn apart."

Christa McAuliffe, who had spent years trapped in the alternate dimension, stepped forward. "We've seen what happens when the timelines cross too much. It starts with small anomalies—objects appearing and disappearing, people shifting between dimensions—but it gets worse. If we don't fix this soon, the two realities will merge, and the result will be... unrecognizable."

The *Challenger* crew had lived through the early stages of this collapse in the alternate dimension, where they had seen entire cities vanish, only to reappear in warped, distorted forms. The idea that both Earths could suffer the same fate sent a cold chill through the rescue team.

"We need to stop the timelines from crossing," Reynolds said, his voice filled with determination. "But how?"

Eliza Langston was already working on a solution. She had spent years studying the rift and the dimensional anomalies, and now, with the data they had gathered from the second explosion, she was beginning to piece together a plan.

"The timelines are tied to the original point of divergence—the *Challenger* explosion," Eliza explained. "If we can lock both dimensions to a stable temporal point, we can stop the timelines from crossing further. But we need to get back to the epicenter of the explosion and use the quantum resonance drive to anchor both realities in place."

Hayes nodded. "It's risky, but it might be our only chance. If we can stabilize both timelines at the moment of divergence, we can prevent the collapse."

The plan was simple in theory but incredibly dangerous in practice. They would need to return to the precise moment when the *Challenger* had exploded—back to the exact point in time where the two realities had first diverged. Once there, they would use the quantum resonance drive to create a temporal anchor, effectively "freezing" both timelines and preventing further merging.

But there was a catch: the instability of the timelines was accelerating. The longer they waited, the closer the two worlds came to merging permanently. And once the timelines fully crossed, there would be no turning back.

As the *Endeavour* approached the epicenter of the rift, the crew felt the weight of the mission pressing down on them. The view outside the shuttle had grown more disorienting with each passing moment—alternate versions of Earth flickered in and out of existence, buildings and landscapes from both realities blending together in an impossible, ever-shifting tapestry.

"We're nearing the original point of divergence," Reynolds said, his hands steady on the controls. "Everyone, prepare for temporal turbulence."

The shuttle shook violently as it passed through the remnants of the rift, the temporal stabilizers humming as they struggled to maintain the ship's position in the fractured space. The epicenter of the explosion appeared before them—a hauntingly familiar sight, the exact moment when the *Challenger* had been torn from their reality, suspended in time like a frozen memory.

"This is it," Eliza said, her voice filled with tension. "We're at the point of divergence."

The crew worked quickly, aligning the quantum resonance drive with the temporal signature of the explosion. The goal was to synchronize both timelines and prevent the crossed realities from spiraling further out of control. But the closer they got to the epicenter, the more unstable everything became.

"We're getting massive temporal distortions," Dana reported, her hands flying across the console. "The timelines are fluctuating wildly. If we don't anchor them soon, they're going to merge."

Reynolds gritted his teeth, holding the ship steady as the quantum resonance drive powered up. Outside, the chaotic energies of the rift swirled faster, pulling fragments of both realities into a single, unstable mass.

"Activate the quantum resonance drive!" Eliza shouted, her voice filled with urgency.

Reynolds hit the switch, and the shuttle shuddered as the drive sent a pulse of energy into the epicenter. The space around them rippled as the timelines began to sync, the fractured realities slowly stabilizing as the temporal anchor locked into place.

But just as they were about to fully stabilize the timelines, the shuttle was hit by a massive shockwave. Alarms blared as the ship lurched sideways, sending the crew scrambling to regain control.

"We've got a problem!" Dana shouted. "The timelines are still crossing! The resonance drive isn't holding!"

Hayes scanned the data, his heart sinking. "It's the second explosion. The energy from the rift is too strong—we're losing control of the stabilization."

Reynolds fought to keep the shuttle in position, but the forces tearing at the ship were too strong. The crossed timelines were merging faster than they could stabilize them, and the result was a chaotic, swirling maelstrom of fractured realities.

"Hold on!" Reynolds shouted, his knuckles white as he gripped the controls.

Outside, the timelines began to overlap in terrifying ways—entire cities flickering between dimensions, buildings crumbling as they shifted between versions of themselves from different realities. The two Earths were colliding, and unless the crew could find a way to stop it, both worlds would be consumed in the chaos.

"We're running out of time!" Eliza shouted. "We need to collapse the rift completely, or the timelines will merge!"

Reynolds glanced at Scobee, who had been silent, watching the chaos unfold. "Francis, we need to make a decision. Do we collapse the rift and risk everything, or do we let the timelines cross and hope for the best?"

Scobee's face was hard, his eyes filled with determination. "We collapse it. If we don't, both realities are doomed."

With no other choice, the crew initiated the final sequence to collapse the rift. The quantum resonance drive surged with power, sending ripples of energy through the fractured space. The timelines buckled, the crossed realities spiraling toward instability.

And then, with a final, deafening pulse, the rift collapsed.

The space around the shuttle went silent as the crossed timelines unraveled, the chaotic energy fading as the quantum anchor took hold. The crew watched in stunned silence as the timelines began to stabilize, the two realities slowly pulling apart.

"We did it," Eliza whispered, her voice filled with disbelief. "We stopped the convergence."

Reynolds let out a long breath, his hands still gripping the controls. "It's over."

Both worlds had been saved—but at a great cost. The rift was gone, the timelines stabilized, but the scars left behind by the crossed realities would take time to heal.

As the *Endeavour* prepared to return home, the crew knew that though they had stopped the collapse, the effects of the convergence would be felt for years to come.

The race against time had been won—but the story was far from over.

Chapter 36: The Sacrifice

The collapse of the rift had stabilized the timelines, but the reality around the *Endeavour* remained fragile. Both universes were still dangerously close to spiraling into chaos, and the crew knew that their victory was only temporary. The quantum resonance drive had done its job, but the delicate balance between the two realities was already beginning to fracture again. The final solution required more than technology—it required a sacrifice.

In the aftermath of the rift's collapse, Dr. Allan Hayes and the rest of the crew worked frantically to assess the damage. The timelines had stopped crossing, but the residual energy from the second explosion was destabilizing both realities. The rescue mission had brought them this far, but they were running out of time.

"We've stabilized the rift for now, but the two realities are still out of sync," Eliza Langston said, her voice filled with tension as she examined the readings. "The quantum resonance drive isn't enough to hold the timelines together. If we don't find a way to permanently anchor them, the rift could reopen—and next time, it'll be worse."

Commander Jack Reynolds, still at the helm, glanced at Eliza. "What are you saying?"

"I'm saying someone needs to stay behind," she replied, her voice heavy with the weight of the decision. "We need a human anchor—someone who can remain in the alternate dimension and stabilize the timelines from within. The rift can't close completely unless both sides are anchored. We've done everything we can from this side, but the final step requires someone to remain in the other reality, to prevent the collapse."

The room fell silent. The enormity of the situation hit everyone at once. They had come so far, fought so hard to save both worlds, but now they were faced with an impossible choice. Someone would have to make the ultimate sacrifice—staying behind in the alternate dimension, cut off from their home and their reality, to ensure the survival of both Earths.

Commander Francis Scobee, who had spent years trapped in the alternate dimension with the *Challenger* crew, stepped forward. His face, etched with years of hardship, was resolute.

"I'll stay," Scobee said, his voice calm and steady. "This world has been my home for years now. I've seen the worst of it, and I know what's at stake. I can do this."

Christa McAuliffe's eyes widened in shock. "Francis, no! You can't stay here. We've been trapped in this dimension long enough—we deserve to go home."

Scobee turned to her, his gaze filled with understanding and a quiet determination. "Christa, we've already given so much to this mission. We came here to save lives, to push the boundaries of exploration. Now we have the chance to save two worlds. If that means I stay behind, then it's a sacrifice I'm willing to make."

Reynolds shook his head, stepping closer. "Francis, there has to be another way. We can figure this out—maybe we can recalibrate the drive, find a way to stabilize both realities without leaving anyone behind."

Eliza's voice broke through the tension, her tone laced with regret. "We've considered every option, Jack. The energy from the second explosion has already destabilized the timelines. The only way to fully anchor them is for someone to remain as a living link, to hold the dimensions in place. Francis is right—this is the only way."

The weight of her words hung heavy in the air. The crew knew it was true, but that didn't make the decision any easier. The room was filled with silent resolve as they processed what needed to be done.

Scobee turned to Reynolds, offering him a small, sad smile. "This is my chance to make things right. I've been stuck in this dimension for years, watching it fall apart, hoping that one day I'd find a way to help. Now I have that chance. Let me do this."

Reynolds' jaw clenched, his heart heavy with the burden of letting a fellow astronaut make such a sacrifice. But deep down, he knew Scobee was right. The *Challenger* commander had lived in the alternate dimension for years, and he understood its fragility better than anyone. He had the strength and the experience to be the anchor that both worlds needed.

"Are you sure?" Reynolds asked quietly.

Scobee nodded. "I'm sure."

The rest of the *Challenger* crew stood in silence, their expressions a mixture of sorrow and pride. They had all fought alongside Scobee, and they knew this decision weighed as heavily on him as it did on them.

"We'll carry your legacy with us, Commander," McAuliffe said, her voice thick with emotion. "But it won't be the same without you."

Scobee smiled softly. "You'll be fine, Christa. You've always been stronger than you realize."

Hayes, who had been standing quietly in the background, finally spoke. "Francis, your sacrifice will save both worlds. We'll make sure you're remembered."

Scobee shook his head. "It's not about being remembered. It's about doing what's right. If staying behind means saving millions of lives—on both Earths—then that's a small price to pay."

The crew gathered around, and for a moment, the weight of their shared experience brought them together. There were no more words to say. The decision had been made, and now it was time to act.

Eliza worked quickly, adjusting the quantum resonance drive to accommodate Scobee's presence as the anchor. The process would be delicate—his life force would become the stabilizing point for the two timelines, ensuring that the rift remained closed and the realities didn't collapse.

Scobee stood by, his gaze distant but resolute, as Eliza explained the process. "Once the drive is activated, you'll be permanently linked to the alternate dimension. You'll stabilize both timelines, but you'll never be able to return to our Earth. The connection will be irreversible."

Scobee nodded. "I understand."

The final preparations were made, and as the team prepared to leave the alternate dimension, Scobee stepped forward, placing a hand on Reynolds' shoulder.

"Take care of them," he said softly.

Reynolds' throat tightened, but he nodded. "We will."

The crew returned to the *Endeavour*, their hearts heavy as they prepared to leave Scobee behind. As the shuttle's engines roared to life and the ship lifted off, they watched as their commander stood on the surface of the alternate Earth, a lone figure against the backdrop of a fractured world.

Inside the shuttle, the silence was deafening as they ascended through the atmosphere. The quantum resonance drive activated, and the timelines began to stabilize. Scobee's presence as the anchor was already working—the two realities were pulling apart, no longer threatening to merge.

As the *Endeavour* broke free of the atmosphere and the rift sealed behind them, they knew that the sacrifice had been made. Francis Scobee, commander of the *Challenger*, had stayed behind to save both worlds.

The shuttle soared back toward their Earth, but the crew's hearts were filled with the weight of what they had left behind. They had succeeded in their mission, but at the cost of one man's life. Scobee would remain in the alternate dimension, forever holding the fragile balance between two worlds.

He had made the ultimate sacrifice to save millions—and in doing so, he had become a legend.

Chapter 37: Closing the Rift

As the *Endeavour* ascended from the alternate dimension, leaving Commander Francis Scobee behind, the crew sat in somber silence. The weight of the decision hung over them all, but they knew it was the only way to save both worlds. Scobee had made the ultimate sacrifice, anchoring the timelines from the alternate Earth, ensuring the rift would remain stable. But now, the final act was upon them—the rift had to be permanently closed, cutting off all connection between the two dimensions, forever.

Dr. Allan Hayes, Eliza Langston, Dana Walker, and the rest of the crew gathered around the controls as the *Endeavour* approached the epicenter of the rift one last time. The quantum resonance drive had been successful in stabilizing the two timelines, but now they needed to deliver the final blow—to seal the rift completely and ensure it could never be reopened.

The view outside the shuttle was surreal, the fractured remnants of the rift still visible as a faint shimmer in the distance. Time and space had calmed since the second explosion, but the threat of instability still lingered. Both Earths were healing, but the rift itself was a scar that had yet to fully close.

Hayes' voice broke the silence. "This is it. Once we close the rift, there will be no going back. The connection between the two dimensions will be severed permanently. We'll lose all contact with the alternate Earth—and with Scobee."

Dana's hands trembled as she adjusted the console. The thought of never being able to reach Scobee again weighed heavily on her heart. He had sacrificed everything to stabilize the rift, and now they would be cutting him off from the only link he had left to his home world.

Eliza Langston, ever the pragmatist, spoke with a quiet determination. "It's what he wanted. Scobee knew the cost. He knew this was the only way to prevent both realities from collapsing."

Reynolds, sitting at the helm, clenched his fists. "I know. But it doesn't make it any easier."

The crew had seen and experienced so much—alternate dimensions, crossed timelines, and averted catastrophes. Yet this moment felt the most personal. Scobee wasn't just another victim of the *Challenger* disaster; he was their friend, their comrade. And now, he would be forever isolated in a reality that wasn't his own.

"Let's make sure we do this right," Reynolds said firmly. "We owe him that much."

The *Endeavour* approached the edge of the rift, the quantum resonance drive primed and ready to initiate the final sequence. Closing the rift would require a precise burst of energy, one that would permanently collapse the dimensional tear and sever any remaining connections between the two worlds. The process was delicate—too much force, and they risked triggering another explosion; too little, and the rift could reopen.

Eliza worked swiftly at her console, inputting the final calculations. "I'm locking in the parameters. Once we initiate the closure, the rift will seal itself over the course of a few minutes. But during that time, the dimensional fabric will be highly unstable. We'll need to maintain our distance to avoid being pulled into the collapse."

Reynolds nodded. "Understood. Let's get this done."

Dana's voice was quiet but resolute. "We're ready."

With everything in place, the crew prepared for the final act. The fate of both realities rested on their ability to close the rift without incident. The quantum resonance drive hummed to life, sending ripples of energy through the shuttle as it prepared to fire the final burst.

But before they initiated the closure, Dana hesitated. Her hand hovered over the controls, her mind racing with thoughts of Scobee—alone, in a world that wasn't his own, forever cut off from the people and the life he had known.

"I just... I wish we could say goodbye," Dana whispered.

Reynolds' expression softened, understanding the pain that came with the loss. "I know. But he knew what he was doing, Dana. He made his peace with it."

Taking a deep breath, Dana nodded, her hand steadying over the controls. "For Scobee."

"On my mark," Reynolds said, his voice steady. "Three... two... one... now."

Dana pressed the button, and the quantum resonance drive fired, sending a powerful pulse of energy toward the rift. The space around them shook as the energy collided with the remnants of the rift, creating a brilliant flash of light that filled the sky.

The rift began to collapse.

Outside the shuttle, the fractured space-time that had once housed the rift started to fold in on itself. The shimmer of the dimensional tear began to shrink, the chaotic energy swirling inward as the timelines finally realigned. It was a beautiful, haunting sight—the slow, deliberate closing of a wound that had torn two worlds apart.

"We've initiated the closure," Eliza said, her voice calm but tense. "The rift is collapsing. Stay sharp, everyone."

The shuttle trembled as the rift's energy continued to swirl, its final death throes sending shockwaves through the surrounding space. But as the rift shrank further, the crew felt an eerie stillness settle over them. It was almost over.

But the personal cost of the moment was palpable. Each member of the crew could feel the weight of the finality—the knowledge that they would never again see or hear from Commander Francis Scobee. He would remain in the alternate dimension, his sacrifice ensuring the safety of both worlds, but forever alone.

As the last remnants of the rift faded into nothingness, the quantum resonance drive powered down, signaling that the dimensional tear had finally been sealed.

"It's done," Eliza announced softly. "The rift is closed."

Reynolds let out a long, slow breath, his grip on the controls relaxing. "We did it."

Dana wiped away a tear as she stared out the window, her heart heavy. "Scobee... I hope you're at peace, wherever you are."

The shuttle crew sat in silence for a long moment, reflecting on the journey they had taken and the sacrifices they had made. They had saved two worlds, averted disaster, and closed the rift that had threatened all of existence. But it had come at a cost—one that would stay with them for the rest of their lives.

Hayes, who had been quiet throughout the closure process, finally spoke. "We'll make sure people remember him. The world will know what he did."

Reynolds nodded. "He'll be remembered. But more than that, his legacy will live on in both worlds. Because of him, both Earths will have a future."

The *Endeavour* began its return journey to Earth, the once fractured sky now clear and calm. The rift was gone, and the two realities had been saved. But the memory of the mission—the loss, the sacrifice, and the bravery of the crew—would stay with them forever.

As the shuttle re-entered the atmosphere and the familiar landscape of their Earth came into view, the crew knew they had done the impossible. They had saved two worlds. And though the cost had been great, they had honored the legacy of the *Challenger* crew in the best way possible—by ensuring that their sacrifice had not been in vain.

The rift was closed, but the story of what had happened would live on. In time, the world would learn of the heroism, the losses, and the ultimate price that had been paid to preserve the balance of the universe.

Commander Francis Scobee, forever bound to the alternate dimension, had given his life to ensure that others could live.

And that was a sacrifice no one would ever forget.

Chapter 38: The Silent Return

The *Endeavour* descended through Earth's atmosphere, its hull glowing faintly as it sliced through the sky toward Cape Canaveral. Inside, the crew remained silent, their thoughts heavy with the weight of what had transpired. They had saved two worlds, stabilized the timelines, and closed the rift, but the cost of that victory would forever be etched in their minds. Commander Francis Scobee was gone, his sacrifice ensuring the survival of both Earths, yet cut off from his own world for eternity.

The surviving members of the *Challenger* crew—Christa McAuliffe, Ronald McNair, and the others—sat quietly, their expressions a mix of relief and sorrow. They had been lost in the alternate dimension for what had felt like years, forced to adapt to a reality where the Cold War never ended and where their very presence was an anomaly. Now, after years of isolation, they were finally returning to their Earth—but it was not the triumphant return they had once dreamed of.

As the *Endeavour* approached its landing, Dr. Allan Hayes and Eliza Langston exchanged knowing glances. The world wasn't ready to hear the truth of what had happened. The dimensions, the rift, the alternate reality—none of it could be revealed. The consequences of such knowledge would be too great, too disruptive to the fragile balance they had fought so hard to protect.

"We all know what's coming," Hayes said quietly, addressing the crew as the shuttle neared its final approach. "When we land, everything we've been through—everything we've seen—will be classified. The world can't know what really happened out there. The public still believes the *Challenger* crew was lost in the explosion, and that's the way it will have to remain."

McAuliffe nodded, her face tired but understanding. "We knew it would come to this. The truth would be too much for people to handle. It's not just about the science—it's about what it would do to the world."

Reynolds' voice was steady, but there was a hint of bitterness behind his words. "We're rewriting history, but I guess we've been doing that since the moment the rift opened. The mission succeeded, but no one will ever know what it really cost."

As the shuttle touched down on the landing strip at Cape Canaveral, the reality of their situation settled in. The *Challenger* crew had survived an impossible ordeal, lived through years in a fractured dimension, and now they were being asked to return to a world that thought they were dead. They would have to disappear from the public eye, their identities concealed, their journey buried beneath layers of classified files.

Government officials and NASA higher-ups were already waiting on the tarmac as the shuttle's hatch opened. Men in dark suits approached, their faces impassive, but their presence made it clear: the story of the *Challenger* would not be told.

As the crew disembarked, they were met with silence. There were no cheers, no celebrations, no media presence. The return of the *Endeavour* was a secret operation, and the handful of personnel who witnessed the landing had been carefully chosen to maintain the secrecy of the mission.

A man in a gray suit, his expression unreadable, stepped forward to greet Hayes and the crew. "Dr. Hayes, Commander Reynolds," he said in a low, formal tone, "I'm sure you understand the gravity of the situation. What happened out there will remain classified at the highest level. The surviving members of the *Challenger* crew will be taken into protective custody for debriefing, and they will be provided with new identities. The official narrative will remain unchanged."

Christa McAuliffe stepped forward, her voice quiet but firm. "And what about us? We've been through hell—trapped in another dimension for years. We deserve the chance to rebuild our lives."

The man in the gray suit regarded her with a measured gaze. "You'll be given new lives, Ms. McAuliffe. Your service has been extraordinary, and we will ensure you are taken care of. But the world cannot know what truly happened. For the safety of both worlds, this story must remain untold."

Ronald McNair, standing beside McAuliffe, crossed his arms, his face hard with frustration. "So, we're ghosts now. We survived, but we don't exist."

The man didn't flinch. "Your sacrifice saved millions of lives. But we cannot risk the consequences of revealing the full truth. You will have new lives, new names. The world will believe you perished aboard the *Challenger*."

Hayes stepped in, his tone calm but resolute. "We knew this was a possibility. The public wouldn't understand what we've seen. The rift, the alternate Earth—it's all too much. But these people deserve more than to be erased."

The man in the suit nodded slightly. "They will be honored, in their own way. The *Challenger* will remain a symbol of sacrifice and exploration. But the details of what happened, the dimensional anomalies, the alternate timeline—that will be buried. History will remember the *Challenger* as it was meant to be remembered: a tragedy that marked the end of an era, but not the one that could have destroyed everything."

The crew stood in somber silence as they absorbed the reality of their situation. They had saved two worlds, but in doing so, they had lost their place in the one they called home. The official narrative would remain intact: the *Challenger* crew had been lost in the explosion, and the details of their extraordinary journey would be sealed away, known only to a select few.

As the man in the gray suit turned to leave, McAuliffe called out, her voice filled with quiet defiance. "Just promise us one thing."

He paused, turning back to face her.

"Don't let them forget what we stood for," she said. "Even if the truth is hidden, don't let the world forget what we gave up for them."

The man nodded solemnly. "That much, I can promise."

With that, the *Challenger* crew was quietly led away, disappearing into the shadows of classified government protocols. They would be debriefed, given new identities, and their lives would begin again—hidden from the world they had saved.

As the shuttle's engines powered down and the landing site was cleared, Dr. Allan Hayes, Commander Jack Reynolds, Dana Walker, and Eliza Langston watched the sky darken overhead. The rift was gone, the timelines stabilized, and both Earths were safe. But the cost of their victory weighed heavily on their hearts.

"It's over," Reynolds said quietly, his voice filled with both relief and regret.

Hayes nodded, but there was a sadness in his eyes. "It's over, but the truth will never be told."

The crew of the *Endeavour*—those who had witnessed the impossible and fought to save two worlds—knew they had done something extraordinary. But the world would never know their names, their stories, or the truth of what had really happened. The *Challenger* would remain a tragic memory, its mission remembered for its courage and loss, but the true journey of its crew would be erased from history.

As they walked away from the landing site, the shadows of secrecy closed in around them. The rift was closed, and so too were the doors to the truth.

And in the silence of that night, the *Challenger* returned home—not with the fanfare of a hero's welcome, but in the quiet, lonely echoes of a story that would never be told.

Chapter 39: A World Changed

The world had been saved, but it wasn't the same world they had left behind. As the remaining *Challenger* crew, NASA officials, and those involved in the mission began to reintegrate into everyday life, they couldn't shake the feeling that something was fundamentally different. The rift had been closed, the timelines stabilized, but the near-convergence of dimensions had left subtle marks on reality—ripples in the fabric of existence that only a few could sense.

Christa McAuliffe, Ronald McNair, and the other surviving members of the *Challenger* crew had been given new identities and quietly relocated to new lives far from the spotlight. Though their faces had once been symbols of hope and courage, they now had to live as ghosts in a world that believed them dead. But something about this new world felt... off.

In the months that followed the closure of the rift, McAuliffe found herself haunted by strange memories—moments that felt out of place, like they didn't belong to her timeline. At night, she dreamed of two versions of Earth, overlapping like a distorted mirror, fragments of her experiences in the alternate dimension bleeding into her dreams. Sometimes, she could hear the distant sounds of Cold War sirens blaring or see flashes of the towering structures from the other Earth's militarized cities. It was as if parts of that other world had followed her home, echoes of a reality she could never fully leave behind.

One morning, while sipping coffee in the small kitchen of her new, anonymous home, she noticed something that sent a chill down her spine. The brand of coffee she had been drinking for years—something she had always relied on as a small comfort—had a different label, a different design. At first, she dismissed it as a minor rebranding, but the changes felt deeper than just packaging. It was the same coffee, but something about it was undeniably different.

McAuliffe wasn't alone in her disquiet. Ronald McNair, now living under a new name in a different city, had begun to experience similar disturbances. He noticed slight but unsettling differences in people's behavior—friends and colleagues who had never mentioned their interest in the Cold War now casually dropped references to it in conversation, as if they had lived through a different history. Buildings he had once walked by on his way to work were now just a little taller, the streets a little narrower. It was subtle, almost imperceptible, but to those who had lived through the dimensional convergence, the world was not quite the same as they remembered.

Dr. Allan Hayes, who had returned to his position within NASA, felt the changes more acutely. His office, once a sanctuary of routine, now seemed unfamiliar. Objects on his desk appeared in different positions each day, even though no one else had access to the room. Files on his computer contained minor discrepancies—words altered, historical facts subtly rewritten. Even the people around him, longtime colleagues, felt different. They looked the same, sounded the same, but their mannerisms, their speech patterns—they weren't quite right.

At first, Hayes tried to rationalize the changes as the product of stress, the toll the mission had taken on him. But the anomalies persisted. It wasn't long before he realized what had happened: the near-convergence of dimensions had altered reality itself, blending subtle aspects of the alternate Earth into their own. The timelines hadn't fully separated after the rift was closed. Instead, they had left behind traces—fragments of the alternate world that had become intertwined with their own.

The same unsettling feeling crept over Eliza Langston as she resumed her work at NASA. Eliza had always prided herself on her precise memory, her attention to detail. But now, even the most mundane aspects of her life felt foreign. At times, she would look at her own reflection and swear that her face looked slightly different—older, sharper, as though the version of herself from the other dimension was slowly surfacing.

"We sealed the rift," Hayes said one afternoon, sitting across from Eliza in a dimly lit conference room. "But we didn't come back to the same world we left."

Eliza, her eyes dark with exhaustion, nodded. "Reality didn't just snap back into place. We closed the tear, but the two dimensions... they touched. There's been some kind of bleed-through."

"How do we explain this?" Hayes asked, his voice laced with frustration. "We can't even talk about it without violating the secrecy agreements. But it's everywhere. Small things—history books with different dates, people remembering events that didn't happen, landmarks changing overnight."

"We're the only ones who know what's really going on," Eliza replied, her voice heavy with the weight of that knowledge. "To everyone else, it's just a glitch in their memory, or they dismiss it as their imagination. But for us, it's like living in a patchwork world—a reality stitched together from two timelines."

The anomalies became more pronounced as time went on. While the general population seemed oblivious to the changes, the small group of those involved in the mission could see the cracks in the fabric of reality. NASA itself had become a nexus for these disturbances—its history subtly rewritten by the presence of the alternate Earth. Old mission reports referenced technologies that didn't exist, or names of personnel who had never worked for the agency.

One day, as Hayes sifted through archived files on the *Challenger*, he came across a document that should not have existed: a detailed report on the alternate dimension. It was filled with technical descriptions of the military-industrial complex from the other Earth, weapons systems that hadn't been part of their own history. The report was dated years before the rift had even opened, as though the two dimensions had always been linked in some way.

"This is what happens when two realities collide," Hayes muttered to himself, feeling the cold certainty of his words.

Christa McAuliffe, now living under her new identity, found herself grappling with more than just altered memories and strange dreams. Occasionally, she would experience moments of intense déjà vu, where the world around her felt like a scene she had already lived—only, in a different version of the timeline. Sometimes, she would catch glimpses of things that weren't there: a Cold War-era poster on a building, a flicker of an unfamiliar skyline in the distance. It was as if fragments of the alternate dimension were still trying to assert themselves.

Ronald McNair, too, felt the weight of these changes. Walking down the street one afternoon, he saw a newspaper stand filled with headlines that made no sense—reports of tensions between the United States and the Soviet Union, stories of secret arms races and diplomatic negotiations that seemed pulled from the alternate dimension. He blinked, and the headlines returned to normal, but the unsettling feeling remained.

The survivors of the mission were now living in a world changed by their actions—a world where the boundaries between dimensions had been blurred. Though they had saved both Earths from destruction, the near-convergence had left its mark, and the changes were permanent.

"We stopped the collapse," Eliza said one evening, speaking to Hayes as they watched the sunset over the NASA headquarters. "But we didn't walk away unscathed. The worlds didn't just touch for a moment—they left imprints on each other."

Hayes nodded solemnly. "We're living in a hybrid reality now, one where both worlds coexist in ways we can't fully understand. We'll never know how much was altered, how much was replaced. All we can do is live with it."

The *Challenger* survivors, along with Hayes, Eliza, and the rest of the team, would spend the rest of their lives navigating this changed world—a place where history itself had been subtly rewritten by the convergence of dimensions. The public would never know the truth. The official story remained intact, the *Challenger* tragedy remembered as it had always been. But for those who had lived through the mission, the world would never feel quite the same.

Reality had shifted, and though the rift was closed, the scars of that near-convergence would linger forever.

Chapter 40: Echoes of the Challenger

Years had passed since the fateful mission to close the rift, and the world had moved on—or so it seemed. The *Challenger* disaster remained in the public consciousness as a tragic chapter in NASA's history, a symbol of human ambition and the risks of exploration. The official story had been carefully maintained, the surviving crew members living out their lives in quiet anonymity under new identities, while the full truth of the mission was buried deep within classified government files. But while the world moved forward, strange phenomena around Cape Canaveral suggested that the rift had never truly been closed.

Dr. Allan Hayes had retired from NASA, but he couldn't fully leave the past behind. He often returned to Cape Canaveral, haunted by memories of the mission and the sacrifice of Francis Scobee. His visits were quiet and private, a pilgrimage to a place where reality had once torn itself apart. He had always believed they had done everything they could, but now, in the twilight of his life, he wasn't so sure. Subtle signs had begun to surface—anomalies that reminded him too much of the dimensional rift they had supposedly sealed.

It started with small disturbances—strange readings from old monitoring equipment left near the original launch site. Over time, the anomalies grew more frequent. Engineers reported glitches in their instruments, brief bursts of energy that didn't match anything in the known physical spectrum. Entire sectors of the space center would experience temporary blackouts, and on more than one occasion, workers claimed to have seen something—an object or figure—that blinked out of existence before they could identify it.

Some dismissed it as superstition, the residual fears of those who knew the history of the site. But others, especially those who had been there for years, felt a growing unease. As the strange occurrences mounted, whispers spread among the old NASA hands—whispers that the rift had never truly been closed, that the dimensional tear had left behind scars in reality, slowly unraveling the fabric of space-time around Cape Canaveral.

One evening, as the sun dipped low over the horizon, casting long shadows across the launch pads, Hayes stood at the edge of the property, staring out over the Atlantic. He had heard the rumors, and while he had tried to dismiss them, the evidence was becoming harder to ignore. He wasn't alone. Eliza Langston, still deeply involved in NASA's research division, had been tracking the anomalies for years, quietly compiling data on the strange occurrences that surrounded the site.

"Do you feel it?" Eliza asked as she approached Hayes, her voice tinged with a quiet tension. "That energy in the air—it's the same as before. Just like when the rift was open."

Hayes nodded, his expression grim. "I've felt it for a while now. We thought we sealed the rift, but something is still here. We stabilized the timelines, but I don't think we ever fully closed the door."

Eliza handed him a tablet, showing recent data she had collected. "These spikes—electromagnetic surges, distortions in local gravity fields—it's all centered around Cape Canaveral. Whatever we did back then, it didn't fix the problem. We stopped the convergence, but the rift is still... echoing."

The term felt eerily appropriate. Echoes of the rift, of the alternate dimension, seemed to ripple through the air around the space center. Unexplained flickers of light, strange sound distortions, even bizarre temperature fluctuations that lasted only seconds but left people unsettled for hours afterward. Some scientists theorized that the space around the site had been fundamentally altered, as if the boundaries between dimensions had become thinner, more permeable.

"We knew there would be risks," Hayes said quietly. "We tampered with forces we didn't fully understand. Closing the rift—it was always a temporary solution. Maybe there's no way to truly seal it."

As the years passed, the phenomena became harder to ignore. Visitors to the Kennedy Space Center occasionally reported seeing flashes of something in the distance—blurred shapes that seemed to shimmer before vanishing. Some claimed to hear faint voices on the wind, distorted and faint, like transmissions from a radio stuck between stations. These reports were dismissed as tricks of the mind, the result of long-standing ghost stories tied to the site. But for those who had lived through the dimensional crisis, the explanations rang hollow.

Christa McAuliffe, living out her quiet, secret life under a new name, couldn't escape the feeling that something was still wrong. Though years had passed since the mission, the memories of the alternate Earth were never far from her mind. She often dreamt of that world—its cold, militarized landscape, the towering structures that stretched into an ominous sky. In her dreams, she was always back there, trying to find her way home.

But sometimes, her dreams felt too real. She would wake with the sensation that she hadn't just been dreaming about the alternate world—she had been there. And when she looked out her window in the early hours of the morning, she could almost see it—the faint outline of another skyline superimposed on the horizon, flickering in and out of view like a distant memory struggling to assert itself.

Ronald McNair experienced similar feelings of dislocation. His life had moved on, but he couldn't shake the sensation that something was pressing in on the edges of his reality. At times, he would be walking down the street and, for the briefest moment, everything would shift—the sky would darken, the buildings would morph into unfamiliar shapes, and he would feel as though he had stepped back into the alternate dimension. These moments were fleeting, but they were enough to remind him that their world had been forever changed by the events at Cape Canaveral.

One night, McNair received a phone call from Hayes, the first time they had spoken in years. "Ron," Hayes said, his voice low and filled with a sense of urgency, "it's happening again. Cape Canaveral—it's not stable. I think the rift... I think it's trying to reopen."

McNair sat in silence for a moment before replying. "I thought we sealed it."

"We thought we did," Hayes replied, "but I don't think the rift ever fully closed. The dimensional fabric around the site is still fragile. I don't know how long we have before something happens, but we need to be ready."

In the years that followed, the strange occurrences around Cape Canaveral became more frequent, more intense. The echoes of the rift grew stronger, and soon, it wasn't just the old NASA veterans who noticed. Tourists began to report seeing strange lights in the sky, and on more than one occasion, entire sections of the space center would experience sudden, unexplained power outages, followed by bursts of static over the intercoms—static that, when played back, seemed to carry faint, distorted voices. Voices that sounded disturbingly familiar.

As the anomalies mounted, NASA quietly ramped up its monitoring efforts, installing new sensors and tracking equipment around the site. Officially, these measures were explained as routine upgrades to the space center's infrastructure, but those in the know understood the truth. The rift, once thought to be sealed, was still there—still waiting, still pulsing with the energy of two worlds that had nearly collided.

One evening, standing alone on the edge of the launch site, Hayes felt a familiar chill run down his spine. The air around him seemed to ripple, the sky above flickering with a strange, almost imperceptible light. He looked up and, for a brief moment, he thought he saw it—an outline of something enormous in the distance, shimmering like a mirage. Then it was gone.

The echoes of the *Challenger*—and of the rift—remained, lingering like a specter over Cape Canaveral. And though the world had moved on, those who had been part of the mission knew the truth: the rift had never truly been closed. The near-convergence of dimensions had left a scar on reality itself, one that could reopen at any moment.

As Hayes walked back toward the complex, his mind raced with possibilities. The rift was still out there, and it wasn't finished with them yet.

The world wasn't safe.

And deep down, Hayes knew—it never would be.

About the Author

Dr. Cassandra Holt is a renowned physicist, historian, and speculative fiction author whose work explores the intersections of science, technology, and the unknown. With a Ph.D. in Quantum Physics from MIT and a lifelong passion for space exploration, Dr. Holt has served as a consultant for multiple aerospace projects and is a frequent speaker at international science conferences.

www.ingramcontent.com/pod-product-compliance
Lightning Source LLC
Chambersburg PA
CBHW061446150726
47987CB00001B/356